GOLF® MAGAZINE

How To **Hit**
Every Shot

GOLF
MAGAZINE

How To Hit Every Shot

The Ultimate Guide to Shotmaking and Scoring

EDITED BY DAVID DENUNZIO

FROM THE
TOP 100
TEACHERS
IN AMERICA

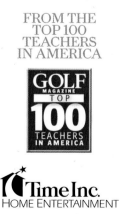

GOLF
MAGAZINE
TOP
100
TEACHERS
IN AMERICA

Time Inc.
HOME ENTERTAINMENT

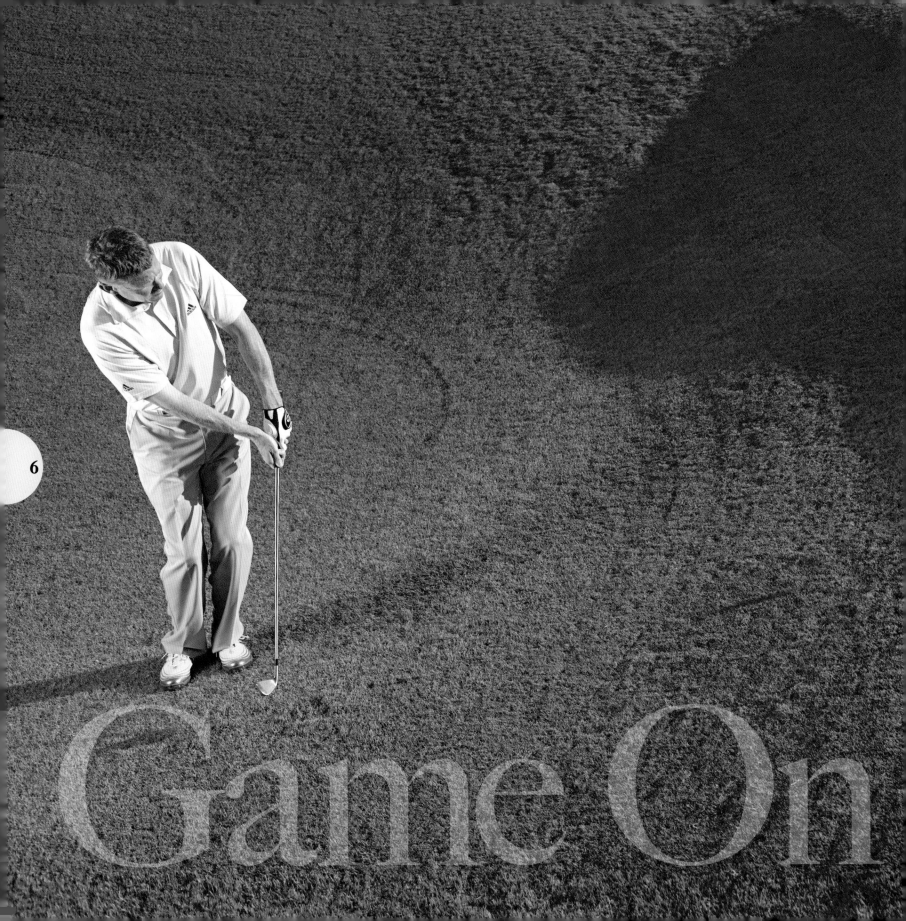

INTRODUCTION

How to Hit Every Shot

The question is the same on every tee box on every hole during every round you play: "How am I going to get *this* ball into *that* cup?" It's a query with deep-rooted ties to the most important element of the game: the number you write on your scorecard. Every golfer likes to spin yarns about big drives and flush 2-irons, but it's your score—the number of strokes it took you to answer the question—that matters.

Of course, it's a question with multiple choices and a thousand correct replies. I'm sure you've come up with a few inventive answers yourself. The variety of options stems from the fact that you're going to hit errant shots now and then and the ball is going to find trouble even when you don't. At these times, your run-of-the-mill full swing won't do you any good. Instead, you need a *shot*— a specialty swing that you place under precise control to make the ball follow a very distinct trajectory. In this book, *Golf Magazine*'s Top 100 Teachers show you how to pull off over a hundred of these shotmaking plays from all over the course. These techniques will help you save par from even the most dire situations. More important, they'll provide you with a clear-cut answer to the question, even when you can't think of one yourself.

David DeNunzio
Instruction Editor, *GOLF Magazine*

Contents

Basics

1

How to Control Your Shots

You don't need a magic wand to make the ball bend to your will. The secret to hitting every shot is hidden in your setup.

NO ONE WILL ARGUE with a straight shot, but you'd be surprised by how few times during a round it's the best option. Plus, most lies don't accommodate a straight ballflight—the majority set you up to produce a very specific trajectory. And that's what makes shotmaking easier than you think. In this chapter you'll learn how changes in your setup—the same ones you're forced to make when you have anything but a perfect lie—affect the way your ball flies, even with your normal swing. Armed with this knowledge, you'll no longer fear adding shape to your shots. You'll accept variations in your setup because you're comfortable with what they do. All that's left is picking the right landing spot, smoothly pulling the trigger and then watching the ball obey orders.

1: CHECK WHERE YOU PLAY THE BALL

Positioning it in the right spot gives you the trajectory you need

Where you play the ball in your stance is a powerful shotmaking tool. The most important thing to remember about ball position is that the further back it is in your stance, the more loft you'll remove from the clubface when it strikes the ball. That's why playing the ball back is associated with lower-trajectory shots.

As you study each of the 101 shots covered in this book, you'll discover that the ones that require you to keep the ball low (or demand ball-first contact at all costs) are played with the ball back in your stance. Conversely, **a forward ball position *adds* loft to the clubface—you'll produce higher trajectories as you move the ball more and more toward the target.**

Ball position also affects direction. A forward ball position promotes open shoulders at impact, making it a useful tool if you want to start the ball left (good for slicers, but bad if you're trying to avoid a hook). A back ball position tends to encourage square or even closed shoulders at impact, making it easier to start the ball out to the right if that's what the shot you're playing calls for.

12

CHECK!
When positioning the ball in your stance, use your heels as your reference points, especially if you flare one foot or both.

BALL BACK
- De-lofts the clubface and produces lower-trajectory shots.
- Good for non-sand escape shots, blasts from the rough and hitting out of a divot.
- Tends to start shots out to the right.

BALL FORWARD
- Adds lofts to the clubface and produces high-trajectory shots.
- Good for tee shots, most sand shots (where you want your swing to bottom out in front of the ball) and uphill lies.
- Tends to start the ball out to the left.

2: CHECK HOW YOU STAND TO THE BALL

Your swing plane depends on it

There's an old rule that when you sole your club behind the ball and take your stance, the distance between your hands and your body should be only slightly farther than when your arms hang straight down. That sets your club on its natural lie angle, which establishes the plane of your swing *[yellow line, right]*. **If you stand closer to the ball, you'll make the shaft more upright and encourage an upright swing *[blue line]*.** Slicers, chunkers and shankers take note. If you stand farther away from the ball, your shaft and swing plane will tend to get flat *[white line]* and your weight will tend to move toward your toes while you swing. You'll have difficulty pivoting around your body and creating speed as a result.

Not many of the shots in this book require you to stand farther from the ball. Some, however, suggest you snuggle up close. You'll see this on shots from the rough (where you want to come down as steep as possible) and from lies where the ball is above your feet (standing close effectively shortens your club).

STEEP SWING

Stand closer to the ball if...
- You have trouble producing sufficient swing speed.
- You frequently hit the ball thin or top it.
- The shot requires you to create a steeper angle of attack.

FLAT SWING

Stand farther away from the ball if...
- You frequently hit slices and shanks.
- You're trying to pick the ball cleanly off the turf.
- The shot calls for you to exaggerate a shallow attack.

Standing closer to the ball encourages a steeper swing.

13

3: CHECK WHERE YOU TAKE YOUR GRIP

Choking down magically turns your club into a completely different weapon

There isn't a rule that says you have to grip the club at the end of the handle. **Choking down is an important shotmaking adjustment.** For starters, it gives you more control of the club since, in essence, you're making it shorter. It also limits how fast you can swing it—good for delicate chip shots around the green, but bad when you've got driver in your hand.

You'll also find that when you choke down on the grip, the shaft gets a little stiffer. It's a subtle way to encourage a lower ballflight.

14

MILD CHOKE

Choke down on the handle a little to...
- Gain extra control.
- Shorten the club.
- Produce slightly less distance with the same club.

MEGA-CHOKE

Choke down on the handle a lot to...
- Stiffen the shaft or to play low-boring specialty shots.
- Hit softer chips with your regular motion.

STANDARD

Grip the club at the end of the handle...
- On regular full swings where you want to get the expected distance from the club in your hands.

4: CHECK HOW HIGH YOU TEE THE BALL

Get it right to dial in the correct launch and curve for the shot at hand

The debate continues: how high should you tee your ball? *[See page 31 for at least one answer].* Like most elements of your setup, there are no absolutes concerning tee height when you're trying to shape shots and make plays. There are, however, some serious causes and effects to consider.

Teeing the ball up higher encourages a flatter swing that will help you produce a right-to-left ballflight. It can also encourage you to swing your clubhead up into the ball through impact and produce a higher launch angle. Lower tee heights usually result in lower trajectories, but also work against you in that they promote the steep angle of attack that's associated with pulls, fades and slices.

HIGH TEE

Tee the ball so that the equator is at the crown if...
- You're looking to hit a draw shot.
- The shot you're playing requires a higher trajectory.
- Your typical mis-hit is a slice.

LOW TEE

Tee the ball below the sweet spot if...
- You're looking to fade the ball.
- You tend to hit hooks (when you're not planning them).
- The shot calls for a shallower angle of attack.

15

5: CHECK YOUR FOOT FLARE

It's not about your stance. It's about your ability to control your hip turn.

The old-school mandate of flaring your front foot while keeping your back foot square is dead. Even the great Ben Hogan, who glorified this stance in his *Modern Fundamentals*, failed to use it during play (he flared both of his feet). That doesn't mean it isn't a useful way to stand. Varying the amount you flare one foot—or even both—is a handy way to create a specific ballflight or trajectory.

The most important thing to know about flaring your feet is that it increases your ability to turn your hips. For that reason, **young and/or flexible golfers are generally better off planting their feet square to the line so that they can keep their hips from over-turning**. If you have limited or even normal flexibility, consider flaring both feet (or at least the one that's on the side where your pivot is limited).

16

RIGHT FLARE
Angle your right foot at address if...
• You can't make a full backswing turn or suffer from a lack of swing speed.
• You typically swing too steep or hit a lot of fat shots.
• The shot calls for you to approach the ball on an inside-out angle of attack.
• You're looking to hook the ball.

LEFT FLARE
Angle your left foot at address if...
• You tend to spin out with your left foot on full swings.
• You typically swing too much from in-to-out or hit hooks
• You want to get the club to lag farther behind your hands and properly hit down on the ball from tight lies.

6: CHECK YOUR FINISH POSITION

How you finish your swing has a lot to say about the shape of your shots

You'd think that with all that goes on in your swing before and during impact, your release and finish are merely afterthoughts. That's hardly the case. In fact, if you think about where you want to finish your swing or, more importantly, *how* you want to finish it, your ability to shape shots and curve the ball on command will skyrocket.

Draws and fades are typically associated with unique release and finish positions (just like specialty shots from sand, where you want to keep the face pointed at the sky after impact). And the more you think about these finish positions and what they feel like, the more apt you are to correctly make the moves beforehand that cause them to happen.

Copy the positions at right to produce the curve or ballflight you're looking for. It's a good idea to rehearse these release and finish arrangements during your practice swings. If you can get to the right spot, the curve you're looking for will take care of itself.

DRAW IT

To produce a right-to-left ballflight...
- Swing the clubhead "out and around" from impact to your finish position.
- Fully extend your right arm.
- Point the toe of the club behind you.
- Get your right hand on top of your left in your release.

FADE IT

To produce a left-to-right ballflight...
- Try to keep your left elbow away from your body at impact.
- Keep your hands ahead of the clubhead all the way into your finish.
- Point the toe of the club at the sky and swing the shaft left of your target.

17

Off The Tee

2

Shape Shots With Your Driver

Long and straight can—and will—get you in trouble. Here's how to select targets and bend the ball into perfect position.

IT TAKES 20 MINUTES in front of your TV watching a Tour event to realize the power of a controlled draw or fade off the tee. A pro's ability to shape drives drops doglegs to their knees and takes trouble immediately out of play, and often allows them to hit two clubs less into the green. Think about that the next time you're reaching for your 4-iron when you could be hitting a six. Plus, your typical tee shot likely has a natural curve; instead of fighting it, why not use it to your advantage? This chapter tells you how to do just that, and arms you with a few tricks and tee-shot options you might never have considered. You'll have to make minor adjustments to your swing, but these are minimal considering the easy birdie opportunities they'll place at your feet.

SHOT 1

A Power Draw You Can Trust

Follow these simple steps to consistently work your tee ball around corners and get more roll

20

What It Is

A right-to-left curving shot (from 5 to 15 yards) that typically gets more roll once it hits the ground because the ball is spinning in the same direction as the target.

When to Use It

As you read this book you'll discover that a draw is a useful shot for many situations (plus, you look cool doing it). On the tee box, it's the go-to option on par 4s that turn hard to the left, where a straight drive will fly through the dogleg and into trouble and clubbing down to a fairway wood or hybrid won't give you the distance to comfortably hit the green.

How to Hit It

For some reason, draw shots are associated with advanced shotmaking, but hitting one is a straightforward, three-step procedure. Just follow the instructions at right.

DIFFICULTY LEVEL

| 0 | 1 | 2 | 3 | 4 | 5 |

This is a difficult shot only if you typically cut across the ball (swing from outside-in). If this is you, take the club back even more to the inside [see Step 2].

IMAGINE THAT
- Picture the draw shape in your mind's eye before you start your swing. The more clearly you see it, the better the chances are you'll execute it.

HANDS FREE
- You don't need to aggressively turn your hands over in your release to curve the ball to the left.
- If you use your normal hand action and exaggerate an inside-out downswing path, the ball will curve.

SPIN ACTION

- Not only will you cut yards off a dogleg with a draw, the ball will roll more once it hits the ground, allowing you to hit an even shorter club into the green.

DANGER!
Since you're aimed right of center, you run the risk of hitting into trouble if you block the shot. Keep turning all the way to your finish.

TEE LEFT

- Teeing the ball on the far left side of the tee box opens more of the right side of the fairway to you and encourages you to swing from the inside-out.

SHOT RECIPE	
CLUB	Driver
AIM	Right of center
STANCE	Square to aim line
BALL POSITION	Standard
SWING	Full backswing, full finish
FEEL	Swing out to the right

HOW TO DRAW IT TO THE CENTER OF THE FAIRWAY

KEY MOVE

Step 1

Stand on the far left side of the tee box, look down the fairway and **pick a target between the center of the fairway and the right rough.** Tee your ball, take your stance and take one final look at your target. It should feel like you're aimed too far out to the right, or that most of the fairway is behind your left shoulder. That's the feeling you're after because you want to swing from inside the target line to the outside.

Step 2

Take the clubhead back low to the ground—very important—and slightly to the inside of your target line. Fight the urge to lift your arms and hands. You should **feel like you're swinging the clubhead around your body** with your hands staying even with or slightly below your right shoulder.

Step 3

From the top, remember where your target is—to the right—and swing under and out toward it. This will keep you from coming over the top and put you on the inside-out track you need. The big mistake here is stopping your body turn and blocking the shot to the right. **Try to point your right shoulder at the target at the finish.** If you end your swing like this, you'll end up in position "A."

21

SHOT

2 Power Fade

Hitting it left-to-right doesn't mean sacrificing distance

What It Is

A left-to-right tee shot that you hit on purpose, not because you left the face open at impact or cut wildly across the ball.

When to Use It

A power fade can be used any time. It's a trustworthy play because it's easier to pull off then a dead-straight drive or one that draws *[see Shot 1]*. It's ideal on holes that turn hard to the right or ones where most of the trouble is up the left side of the fairway.

How to Hit It

Old-school instruction tells you to open your stance, point your clubface at where you want the ball to end up and then swing along your stance line. That's a lot to think about. There's a much easier way, and all you have to do is make your normal swing. *Follow the instructions at right:*

SWING EASY
- Don't try to kill the ball. Increasing your swing speed increases your chances of your hands turning over and hooking the ball into the junk.

AIM LEFT
- Pick a spot between the center of the fairway and the left rough—that's the line your shot travels on before it turns right.

TEE RIGHT
- Tee the ball on the right-hand side of the tee box.
- This gives you more room to play your drive to the left before it curves back to the center.

22

HOW TO HIT FOR POWER (AND AVOID TROUBLE ON THE LEFT)

Step 1

Take aim at the left side of the fairway
Tee your ball on the right side of the tee box and aim your feet slightly left of the center of the fairway.

✓

CHECK!
Tee your ball low for this shot. It will encourage you to swing level through impact and guard against hitting a pull hook.

KEY MOVE

23

Step 2

Open the face
Before you take your grip, rotate the clubface open a few degrees and then secure your hold. Play the ball one ball's width forward of normal.

Step 3

Hit the outside
Make your normal backswing and downswing. Your setup and open face automatically create the left-to-right curve you're planning on. It helps if you aim for the outside quadrant of the ball. Striking here increases the likelihood that the ball will fade back to the center of the fairway.

SHOT RECIPE	
CLUB	Driver
AIM	Left of center
STANCE	Square to aim line
BALL POSITION	Slightly forward of standard
SWING	Full backswing to full finish
FEEL	Hit the outside half of ball

DIFFICULTY LEVEL

0	1	2	3	4	5

This is the easiest tee shot to hit, and a good one to use on the first few holes if you didn't have time to warm up before your round.

3

Extra-High Drive

Blast it way up in the air to ride the breeze down the fairway

What It Is

A tee shot that launches higher than normal. This usually cuts off some distance from your drive, but in the right situation this shot can give you 15 extra yards.

When to Use It

On a tee box with a decent wind at your back. It's also a great option when you need to blow it over trees if you're not comfortable hitting a draw or fade on a dogleg.

How to Hit It

Common advice tells you to tee the ball higher, but that's probably why you pop it up when you try to hit it high. Keep your tee height the same, but play the ball forward of where you normally tee your driver and take an extra-wide stance with your weight favoring your right foot [see steps at right]. As you swing down from the top, try to hang back on your right side a little longer. Hanging back like this automatically creates a higher launch. And the best part is, you don't have to alter your swing or think about hitting up on the ball.

DIFFICULTY LEVEL

| 0 | 1 | 2 | 3 | 4 | 5 |

You can hit high shots with your everyday swing. The minor adjustments you need are easy to make and actually guard against pop-ups.

HEAD BACK
- Hang back on your right side on your downswing so that your head is over your right kneecap at impact.

EVEN STRIKE
- Don't try to hit up on the ball—that's a recipe for pop-ups.
- Make your normal move through impact and let the forward ball position and your hang-back move take care of launch.

SHOT RECIPE	
CLUB	Driver
AIM	At target
STANCE	Extra-wide
BALL POSITION	Off left toe
SWING	Full backswing, full finish
FEEL	Hang back on right side

HOW TO BLAST IT HIGH

Step 1
Sole your clubhead behind the ball with your feet together.

Step 2
Set your left foot even or just slightly ahead of the ball.

Step 3
Step to the right with your right foot and create a slightly wider stance (one foot's width wider).

HIPS TURN

- Even though you're trying to hang back on your right side, get your hips turning toward the target like normal.

FINISH LEFT

- If you hang back just the right amount, you'll automatically knock the ball higher and the momentum of your swing will pull you into a standard finish with your weight over your left foot (make a few practice swings to get this right).

KEY MOVE

Step 4
Your setup puts you more over your right side—maintain that arrangement on your backswing. You've done it right if your head is over your right knee at the top.

Step 5
As you come back down, hang back on your right side. Don't overdo it—just make sure your head is still over your right knee when you strike the ball.

The Rules Guy

Shotmaking by the Book

Food for Thought on Provisionals

Your extra-high drive didn't clear the trees you were trying to blast over, or your draw turned into a smother hook, and now you fear your tee ball is lost or out-of-bounds. You're an optimist by nature (you have to be if you continue to subject yourself to the indignities of this game) so you announce to your playing partners, "I'm hitting a provisional" (from the Latin *provid*, which means "hitting three"). Hitting a provisional certainly is your prerogative, and announcing it to your partners using those exact words is an important first step. **If you don't make the announcement, your provisional automatically becomes the ball in play.**

If you find the original ball and it's in play, you must play it and pick up your provisional shot. No penalty stroke is assessed. If you can't find your first, you must play your provisional. Unfortunately, you're penalized stroke and distance (the penalty stroke plus your shot) so you're now hitting your fourth shot.

If you decide not to hit a provisional off the tee and fail to find the original ball, you must high-tail it back to the tee and re-hit with a one-stroke penalty, so it's a good idea to play a provisional shot if there's any doubt if the first ball is in play. Just don't abuse the rule; a provisional is a time-saver, not a means to get a few practice swings in.

25

SHOT

4 Low Drive

Move the ball back in your stance to crush it low

What It Is
A drive kept intentionally low.

When to Use It
On blustery days when the hole you're playing runs straight into the teeth of the wind. Hit it high here and the ball will balloon up into the air and fall way short of your normal distance.

How to Hit It
Make a simple ball-position change and keep the tempo of your swing the same. For a typical drive, you should play the ball off your left armpit. To keep the ball low into the wind, move the ball back so you're playing it off the left side of your chest, or the logo on your shirt. One final adjustment: forward-press your hands slightly toward the target to slightly hood the clubface. Now you're in business.

DIFFICULTY LEVEL

| 0 | 1 | 2 | 3 | 4 | 5 |

It's just a change in ball position. Plus, you get to swing easier than normal.

WIND CHECK
- If it's in your face, play this low shot. If it's at your back, hit your drive extra high [see Shot 3].

KEY MOVE

LOGO LOW
- On normal drives you set up with the ball played off your left foot. To keep it low, move the ball back so it's off the logo on your shirt.

NORMAL DRIVE SETUP
1. Position the ball off your left armpit so you catch it slightly on the upswing.
2. Set your hands and the clubshaft even with the inside of your left thigh.
3. Sole the clubhead flat on the ground with its normal amount of loft.

TOE IT IN
- At address, toe in your clubface slightly (only 1 or 2 degrees). Hooding the clubface like this guarantees you don't add loft at impact and launch the ball too high into the air.

SHOT RECIPE	
CLUB	Driver
AIM	At target
STANCE	Standard
BALL POSITION	Slightly back (off shirt logo)
SWING	Full backswing to full finish
FEEL	Like you're swinging at 80%

LOW-DRIVE SETUP
1. Position the ball off your left chest or the logo on your shirt.
2. Set your hands and the clubshaft even with the center of your left thigh.
3. Hood the clubhead slightly (toe in) to ensure a lower ballflight.

DANGER!
Don't try to kill the ball on this shot—the old line about "when it's breezy, swing easy" does hold true.

SHOT 5 The Stinger Long Iron

This low-flying laser is key on tight par 4s and on tee shots into the wind

What It Is

A stinger is a low-flying drive you hit with one of your long irons. It won't fly as far as shots hit with your driver, but it will spin less, making it easier to control.

When to Use It

When you're hitting into the wind or you need to be super-accurate on a tight driving hole and you can sacrifice some distance off the tee.

SHOT RECIPE	
CLUB	3-iron
AIM	Standard
STANCE	Stand closer to ball
BALL POSITION	Slightly back
SWING	At 70 % speed
FEEL	Stiff-wristed short swing

DIFFICULTY LEVEL

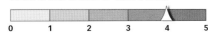

0   1   2   3   4   5

You hit a stinger with a 3-iron, which is probably your weakest club, so this shot is for advanced players only.

HOW TO STING IT DOWN THE FAIRWAY

Step 1
Get forward
Set up so that you're slightly in front of the ball. (Your shirt buttons should be just ahead of the ball at address.)

Step 2
Get closer
Grip down one inch. This allows you to stand closer to the ball, which helps you hit down on it and keep it low.

Step 3
Get shorter
Make a shoulder-high to shoulder-high swing. The shorter the swing, the lower the ballflight.

Step 4
Get smooth
Lead the clubhead into impact with your hands. Swing at about 70 percent—harder swings tend to increase loft.

KEY MOVE

Step 5
Get bowed
Make sure your left wrist is bowed at impact. This delofts the club. If your wrist breaks down, you'll add loft to the shot.

Step 6
Get compact
Make a three-quarter follow-though. A full finish equals a high trajectory, so make sure to cut it short.

27

SHOT 6 How to Drive the Green

On short par 4s, hitting driver is the right choice for bombers and bunters alike

The Situation
There are bunkers left and right of the green on this uphill 280-yard par 4. Dense rough surrounds the green, but the front is open.

The Solution
Let that big dog eat! Almost 90% of the Top 100 Teachers in America recommend you hit driver in this situation and go for the green in one.

How to Dominate Short Par 4s
Check the clues at right. If you have a green-light situation, consult Shot 8 for how to get the most yards out of your driver.

28

IF YOU'RE A BIG HITTER

The Top 100 Teachers say...
87% Go for it!
11% Lay up to a comfortable yardage
- A good player gets up-and-down from 100 yards about 30%, but can do it 50% from a greenside bunker and nearly 60% from within 30 yards. Going for the green ups the chances you'll make birdie. Plus, it's more fun.

IF YOU'R ACCURATE, BUT NOT LONG

The Top 100 Teachers say...
87% Hit driver
13% Hit a fairway wood or hybrid
- Since you're likely to hit the fairway with any club you choose, you might as well get as much distance out of the shot as possible. You don't get many chances to hit sand wedge on a par-4 approach shot, so take advantage of it.

The upslope will make your approach shot fly higher and land softer.

If the pin is tucked in any of the four corners, play to the center to avoid a tricky second shot.

There's no shame in hitting two 7-irons when you card a "3."

IF YOU STRUGGLE WITH LONGER CLUBS

The Top 100 Teachers say...
66% Hit 6-iron from the tee
34% Hit a hybrid
- Determine the longest club you can hit that will leave you a comfortable full-swing distance from the pin. If that club is a 6-iron, and the landing area is clear, then swing away. If not, drop down to a 7-iron.

DIFFICULTY LEVEL

| 0 | 1 | 2 | 3 | 4 | 5 |

Making a bold decision is easy, but you still need to execute. For help on hitting extra-long drives, see page 30.

SHOT RECIPE	
CLUB	Driver
AIM	At target
STANCE	Standard
BALL POSITION	Standard
SWING	Standard
FEEL	Confidence in your selection

7
Drive From an Angled Tee Box

Focus on the target, not your ball, so you don't get fooled again

The Situation

The tee box you're standing on faces away from your landing area. In fact, it points to the left rough. Be careful: It's a trick. Many players instinctively aim where the tee box is facing, so this hole is designed to fool you.

The Solution

The key to keeping your drive in the fairway is to pick an intermediate target just a few feet in front of the ball that's in line with your actual target. Then forget about the tee box and focus on hitting the ball over that intermediate target. *Follow the steps at right:*

DIFFICULTY LEVEL

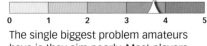

| 0 | 1 | 2 | 3 | 4 | 5 |

The single biggest problem amateurs have is they aim poorly. Most players aim their body at the target instead of the clubface. A tricky tee box just compounds the problem.

HOW TO AVOID TROUBLE ON AN ANGLED TEE BOX

Tee box points here. Your target is here.

Step 1

Stand on the tee box and figure out where you want to land your drive, picking a target in the distance and an intermediate target just a few feet away on the same target line.

KEY MOVE

Step 2

Tee the ball just behind your intermediate target. You should be able to picture an imaginary line running straight from your ball through the intermediate target to the actual target in the distance.

Step 3

Set up square to the ball with your body lines parallel to the target line.

Step 4

Forget about hitting the ball at your actual target. Focus on drilling the ball over your intermediate target.

F.Y.I.
Just like you line up the brand name on your ball when you putt, line up the name of the ball with your target line when you drive.

SHOT RECIPE	
CLUB	Driver
AIM	At target
STANCE	Parallel left of target line
BALL POSITION	Standard
SWING	Full back to full finish
FEEL	Drive over intermediate target

29

SHOT

8 The Big Bomb!

Three easy moves give you extra speed where you need it most

What It Is
A tee shot not just hit hard, but *creamed*.

When to Use It
You'd think on every tee box, but on most holes, consistency—not extra yards—should be your goal. When the hole stretches out or you need a big drive in order to go for a par-5 green in two, however, the Big Bomb is your best bet.

How to Hit It
There isn't a magic formula for extra distance—driving requires that your follow some hard, fast rules. Break these and you may never see the ball you're hitting again. Your goal is to make a fundamentally sound swing but at a higher rate of speed. There are 3 key areas you can focus on to gas up your motion. Capitalize on these and you'll get the extra miles per hour you need without having to swing out of your shoes.

DIFFICULTY LEVEL

0	1	2	3	4	5

You only need to focus on 3 areas, but if you aren't close to perfecting them on normal swings, you'll have difficulty here, too.

SHOULDER POWER
- Turn them so your back faces the target at the end of your backswing.
- This gives you more time to build up speed.

WRIST POWER
- Keep your hands and wrists soft during your downswing.
- This move helps you create clubhead lag.

HIP POWER
- Turn them aggressively to the left on your downswing.
- This move creates whip-like speed through impact.

SHOT RECIPE	
CLUB	Driver
AIM	At target
STANCE	Standard
BALL POSITION	Standard
SWING	Big turn back, fast turn through
FEEL	Soft wrists

30

SPEED FACTOR 1: FULL BACKSWING TURN

Make sure you complete your shoulder turn during your backswing. The more you turn your shoulders going back, the more time they'll have to pick up speed going forward. You'll know your shoulder turn is full when you feel your left shoulder turn underneath your chin and your back is pointing directly at the target.

Don't Do This
Cutting your shoulder turn short robs you of speed.

Do This
Turn your left shoulder all the way under your chin.

SPEED FACTOR 2: SOFT WRISTS

During your downswing, keep your wrists soft and tension-free. This allows you to retain the angle between your left arm and the shaft (lag angle) deeper into your downswing. The longer the club lags behind your hands [photo, below right], the more speed you'll have at the bottom of your swing when you release the club through the hitting zone.

KEY MOVE

Don't Do This
Tight wrists lead to an early release.

Do This
Keep your wrists soft to retain your lag angle.

SPEED FACTOR 3: HIP TURN

As you approach impact, make sure you're moving your hips and legs strongly toward the target. This, along with your soft wrists, allows your left arm to lead the clubhead into the ball. This is a key element of power—do it correctly and the club will whip through the ball at maximum speed.

EXTRA LESSONS

Our exclusive test proves you get more yards when you tee the ball high

The Experiment
Twenty-seven golfers aged 25 to 71, with handicaps ranging from scratch to 29, hit 10 drives at the following tee heights (low: top edge of ball even with top of clubhead; medium: equator of ball even with the top of the clubhead; and high: bottom of ball even with the top of the clubhead). Only the best five out of each player's 10 drives at each tee height were recorded.

The Analysis
Carry distance and other data were measured by a launch monitor. Accuracy was also recorded: drives that landed in the fairway were scored higher than those that landed in the rough.

The Results
Carry distance for mid and high tee heights was significantly longer than the low tee height, largely an effect of the higher tees promoting higher launch angles and less spin. The high tee height provided the most distance, giving players an average of 12 yards more carry per drive than the low tee height.

The perfect tee height—bottom of the ball at top of clubface. Tee your ball slightly above the crown.

HANDICAP	CARRY DISTANCE (YDS)		
	Low Tee	Mid Tee	High Tee
Low (0-9)	211.64	219.62	222.92
Mid (10-19)	171.46	177.84	179.84
High (20+)	160.85	174.15	178.24

31

SHOT

9
High-Accuracy Drive

Make your own tee, then make the ball go straight

What It Is
A low-flying, low-spinning tee shot that you hit with your driver. This baby almost always finds the fairway.

When to Use It
You're on the tee of a narrow par 4 with trouble left and right, and you can get away with hitting short of your full driver distance. This shot is also useful when the wind is in your face and you can't afford for it to push the ball back.

How to Hit It
Kick up the ground to make a "turf-tee" and use it as a launching pad to drive the ball low and hard. This shot uses the same principles as the driver off the deck [Shot 92], but with a slight advantage because the ball is resting on soft turf. Both shots come off with very little spin, making them less prone to curve off line if you catch them solid.

DIFFICULTY LEVEL

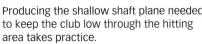

| 0 | 1 | 2 | 3 | 4 | 5 |

Producing the shallow shaft plane needed to keep the club low through the hitting area takes practice.

32

ADD CONTROL
- Choke down for extra control and play the ball way back of where you normally tee your driver to encourage a lower ballflight.

LOW RIDER
- Since the ball sits below the level of your normal tee height, keep the clubhead low through impact.
- Feel like you're extending your arms fully from their sockets, or like you're hitting an extra-hard punch.

TURF TEE
- Tee your ball on a mound fashioned from dirt you kick up on the tee box.
- This low tee takes a ton of spin off the shot, but isn't so low that you can't loft the ball off of the turf.

SHOT RECIPE	
CLUB	Driver
AIM	At target
STANCE	Square to target
BALL POSITION	Toward center of stance
SWING	Full back to full finish
FEEL	Like it's an elongated pitch

HOW TO NEVER MISS OFF THE TEE

Lift...

...drop...

...place.

Step 1

Make a "turf-tee"
Kick your heel down on the tee box to dislodge a little dirt, mold the dirt into a platform and "tee" the ball on top of it. This low tee automatically takes spin off the ball while the back ball position (see Step 2) de-lofts the club, giving you a low, straight screamer.

Step 2

Set up in a low-trajectory stance
Address the ball to promote a low-driving shot by playing it about two clubhead widths back of where you normally tee your driver [*photo,right*]. Choke down on the club about an inch; you'll be more able to control the face with a shorter club.

Step 3

Stay low through the impact area
Make your regular driver swing, but focus on keeping the club low through impact [*photo, left*]. You should feel like you're hitting an elongated punch shot.

Don't Forget About Your Hybrid

The club that seems to do everything is also a great choice for hitting low-running draws on tight holes

If the thought of plowing your driver through a man-made turf-tee isn't your idea of a safe play, then turn to your trusty, stainless-steel friend, the hybrid. Your lowest-lofted model can be modified at address to give you a low, running hook that covers 200 yards, making it a go-to option on tight driving holes.

Address
Aim your body down the right edge of the fairway and close the face slightly so it points down the middle of the fairway. Move the ball back in your stance about one ball's width from where you normally tee your hybrid.

Backswing
On your backswing, try to make the biggest turn your flexibility will allow (flare your right foot at address to give you a few more degrees of upper-body turn). A strong turn sets you up to swing on the proper inside-out path on your downswing.

Downswing
On the way back down, keep your left arm soft so that your forearms can rotate and turn the club over through impact (the move that puts draw spin on the ball). It helps to think about unfolding your left elbow and pointing it at your left hip as your club nears contact.

Do it correctly and the ball will come out hot, low and with enough draw spin to curve it back to the fairway.

33

From The Fairway

CHAPTER

3

Hit the Green From Any Lie

Slope and the elements are against you, but they're no match when you've got 30 pin-seeking approach shots in your bag

PERFECT TEE SHOTS lead to easy approaches, but sometimes the ball finds a spot that, while smoked off the tee and still on the short stuff, leaves you with an awkward stance, and for most golfers that's a recipe for disaster. Other times your lie is great, but there's an obstacle in your way or the pin is tucked so ridiculously tight that you risk landing in a bunker or water hazard if you go straight at it. The good news is that there's more than one way to get the ball on the green. In fact, there are dozens, and if you acquaint yourself with even a fraction of these options, you'll be prepared for anything the course throws at you. That makes every situation a birdie situation, and separates you from the other golfers just hoping to save par.

SHOT

10 Ball Above Your Feet

You won't get as much distance, so opt for a fairway wood or a hybrid for an easier shot to the green

The Situation

You kept your tee shot in play, but the ball came to rest on a sloping section of the fairway. When you take your stance the ball is above your feet.

The Problem

The slope will force your ball to the left. Also, if you make your normal swing, you'll come in too steep and your swing will bottom out before the ball, which causes fat shots, thin shots and all sorts of other bad results.

DIFFICULTY LEVEL

| 0 | 1 | 2 | 3 | 4 | 5 |

The ball-above-your-feet lie is the easiest of all uneven lies. Since the typical golfer struggles with a slice, this lie actually is easier to hit since you're less likely to come over the top.

The Solution

The first thing you need to do is take the right club. For a long approach shot, grab a fairway wood or a hybrid and aim about 10 yards right of your target. If you're playing a short iron, you'll need to aim 15-20 yards left of the target because irons tend to hook far more than fairway woods and hybrids *[see right for more information]*. Make sure to swing more around your body to match the slope of the hill—your normal upright swing will come in too steep.

OFFSET SLOPE
- Aim 10 yards right of your target to offset how the slope will pull your shot to the left.

POWER DOWN
- Go at this one at about 80% speed. If that means using a longer club, then use it.

BATTER UP!
- When the ball is above your feet, think "baseball swing" instead of "golf swing."

SHOT RECIPE	
CLUB	One more than the distance
AIM	10 yards to the right
STANCE	Standard
BALL POSITION	Standard
SWING	80% power
FEEL	Like swinging a baseball bat

36

HOW TO CRUSH A BALL ABOVE YOUR FEET

KEY MOVE

DO THIS

- Swing your club back on a flatter plane. There's not much to the shot other than making sure you don't come in too steep.
- Since swing plane is a difficult concept, it's helpful to think about swinging a baseball bat. Feel like you're swinging around yourself. Follow the orange line, not the white one [right].

F.Y.I.
Hitting a ball above your feet is a good way to cure a slice because it forces you to make a more inside-out swing.

Stay below your normal swing plane.

DON'T DO THIS

- The secret to executing this shot is to match your swing plane to the slope.
- The lie angle on a typical fairway wood combines with the slope to produce a much flatter swing plane. Rise above it and you'll have to make too many adjustments on the way down to avoid hitting fat.

The ideal swing plane flattens out on a slope because the hill decreases the effective lie of the club.

HOW TO AIM FROM A SIDEHILL
Let the club in your hands point you in the right direction

You have a sidehill lie with the ball above your feet about 180 yards from the pin. You know the ball is going to curve to the left, so you grab your 4-iron and aim 10 yards right of your target. Unfortunately, the ball curves only five yards to the left. You had the right idea—a sidehill lie with the ball above your feet will cause your ball to curve to the left, but the amount of curve depends on the club in your hands. **Because they have more loft and a more upright lie, short irons are more affected by slope than long irons.** Conversely, long irons—like the 4-iron you're using in this situation—are less affected by slope [check the difference in the photos below]. Because of this difference, you don't need to aim so far to the right when you're swinging your mid to long irons from this lie.

NOTE: The sidehill effect on aim occurs even on small pitches and chips. If you typically use your sand wedge in these situations and often pull the ball left of the hole, drop down to a less-lofted club, like your pitching wedge or 9-iron.

37

From a steep sidehill lie, the face of a mid-iron will point slightly left of the target.

A short iron points much farther left of the target from the same lie—you'll have to aim farther right.

SHOT 11

Ball Below Your Feet

You need to get down, down, down to get this one on

The Situation

You're within easy mid-iron distance to the green, but the ball sits below your feet when you take your stance. Balance is an issue, but the real problem is that the ball is farther away from you than normal.

The Solution

Lower your body to the ball so you can make solid contact. Also, aim left. The slope will make this ball curve to the right, and the longer the club you use, the more right it will bend.

Swing at 70 percent and take one more club than normal. An easier swing will help you maintain your balance. Plus, they don't call it a long iron for nothing—that extra half-inch between your 6-iron and your 7-iron will help you get down easier.

DIFFICULTY LEVEL

| 0 | 1 | 2 | 3 ▲ | 4 | 5 |

Most people practice only off level lies, so it can be difficult to maintain your balance on this shot.

You won't keep your posture if you bend only from your waist.

Bend from your knees so you don't have to bend so much from your hips.

HOW TO CATCH A BALL BELOW YOUR FEET CRISP

DON'T DO THIS...

Don't just bend from your waist or hips to get down to the ball. The more your upper body bends down toward the ground the more difficult it will be to hold your posture on your downswing. The likely result: You'll raise up and catch the ball extremely thin or send it squirting off to the right.

F.Y.I.
The half-inch gap between irons means your 3-iron is 4 inches longer than your 9-iron (why long clubs are easier from this lie).

DO THIS...

At address, take a wider stance than usual and add more knee flex. These simple moves lower your body and bring you closer to the ball.

ADJUST AIM

- Where you aim depends on the club.
- For a 4-iron, aim 15 yards more left to offset the effect of the slope. However, for a sand wedge, you only need to aim a few yards left.

REVERSE CHOKE

- Make sure you're holding the club at the very end of the handle.
- You need every inch of your club to get down to the ball.

KEY MOVE

STAY PUT

- When you swing, your main focus should be to maintain the posture you had at address.
- Stay in the shot and try to take a little divot. If you straighten up, you have no chance to get down to the ball.

39

SHOT RECIPE	
CLUB	One more than normal
AIM	Left of target
STANCE	Outside shoulder-width
BALL POSITION	Standard
SWING	At 70% speed
FEEL	Stay in your address posture

SHOT

12 Ball Severely Below Your Feet

This lie requires you to take your swing to the vertical limit

AIM LEFT
- You're going to produce a ton of left-to-right sidespin from this lie.
- Aim left of the target (10 yards for a mid-iron, 15 yards for a long iron).

GET VERTICAL
- Notice how much lower the right shoulder is than the left, and how the opposite occurs during your backswing [photo, Step 2].
- This "high-low" shoulder relationship is key to producing a very vertical swing (the kind you need

STAY DOWN
- Your chances of making solid contact are good if you stay in your address posture.
- Raise up on this shot and you'll catch the ball very, very thin.

40

SHOT RECIPE	
CLUB	Mid-iron
AIM	10 yards left of target
STANCE	Weight on heels
BALL POSITION	Center
SWING	Vertical back and through
FEEL	Chest on top of the ball

The Situation
You're within easy mid-iron distance of the green, but the ball is on a downslope in the right rough. When you go to take your stance, the ball is severely—as in a solid foot—below your feet. You feel like you're going to shank it right from the start.

The Solution
First, accept the fact that you might not be able to reach the green from this lie—but you can get close. Like all sloping lies, the key to hitting a good shot when the ball is below your feet is to match your swing plane to the shape of the hill.

DIFFICULTY LEVEL

| 0 | 1 | 2 | 3 | 4 | 5 |

As you'd expect, this is a very easy shot to hit thin. A good image to have is that you're keeping your chest the same distance from the ball from the start of your swing through impact.

HOW TO NIP IT FROM WAY BELOW YOUR FEET

KEY MOVE

Step 1

Bend from your hips more than normal to get the clubhead behind the ball. It's a good idea to take a longer club than what you need to help you get all the way down. Aim a good 10 yards left of your target—this ball will fade.

Step 2

Make as vertical a backswing as possible (it should come easy since you're bent over so much). Feel like your clubhead is riding a Ferris wheel and try to get your hands above your head.

Step 3

Swing sharply down (as steep as you did on your backswing) and hold your posture—no raising up or dipping down allowed. If you feel the face opening, don't force it closed (you aimed left to compensate for the ensuing fade).

Step 4

Continue the steep theme in your through-swing, moving the club up sharply after you make contact with the ball. Shift your weight forward from your right-foot toes to the heel on your left foot to maintain your balance.

SHOT

13 Ball Severely Above Feet

Here's one shot where it's okay to stand straight up

The Situation

In defiance of gravity, the ball has come to rest on a sideslope. (If the grounds crew mowed more often the ball would have rolled down to a flat lie!) When you take your stance, the ball is higher than your knees.

The Solution

Many of the keys used to catch the ball when it's just slightly above your feet *[see Shot 10]* apply in this situation. Just apply them to an extreme.

DIFFICULTY LEVEL

| 0 | 1 | 2 | 3 ▲ | 4 | 5 |

This one isn't so tough. Just make sure to plan for the hook ballflight and remain standing tall.

SHOT RECIPE	
CLUB	One more than the yardage
AIM	15 yards right of target
STANCE	Weight on toes
BALL POSITION	Center
SWING	Flat and full back and through
FEEL	Swing right arm across chest

HOW TO BAT IT OFF A HILL

With the ball so far above your feet, your posture will be very tall. (You also may need to choke down on the grip an inch or two.) Check the distance to the green, and take an extra club. The hill will cause your ball to hook, so aim a good 15 yards to the right.

The secret to this lie is to remain standing tall. You can take a full hack if you need to, but the harder you swing, the greater the chances are that you'll lean into the hill to maintain your balance. That's when you catch the ball fat.

Try to finish your swing standing as tall as you did at address. To ensure that your swing stays sufficiently flat, think about swinging your right arm across your chest after impact.

Swing your right arm across your chest after impact.

41

SHOT

14

Approach Shot From an Upslope

This isn't a tough lie—it's a man-made launching pad!

DIFFICULTY LEVEL

| 0 | 1 | 2 | 3 | 4 | 5 |

If you swing the right club and don't try to do too much with it, your chances of hitting the green are very good.

42

The Situation

Your drive missed the fairway and landed in some light rough. The lie is good, but you're on an upslope. When you take your stance, your left foot is much higher than you're right, and you feel like you're going to tumble down the hill if you make your regular full swing. You don't want to hit a safe pitch back to the fairway because you're just a mid-iron away from the green.

The Solution

Bag any thoughts of hitting a recovery shot—this isn't a lie that should stop you from getting on in regulation. The adjustments you need to make are easy, including the most important: Hitting two clubs more than the listed distance.

BALL IN FRONT
- Since the ground is higher on the target-side of your stance, play the ball forward so you won't dig your club into the hill.

✓

CHECK!
Take a wider stance for any uneven lie. You're not use to swinging from slopes, and you'll benefit from the extra stability.

ARM POWER

- Gravity won't allow you to move your lower body toward the target like it does on your full swing, so make it an all-arms swing with just a touch of lower-body turn.

CLUB DOWN

- The hill adds loft. Correctly swinging up the slope does, too, turning your 5-iron into a 7-iron.
- Regardless of the distance to the green, use two clubs more than what you normally use for that yardage to counteract the extra loft created by the upslope.

SHOT RECIPE	
CLUB	Two clubs more than yardage
AIM	Slightly left of target
STANCE	Extra wide
BALL POSITION	Slightly forward of standard
SWING	¾ backswing to ¾ finish
FEEL	Hit the shot with all arms

HOW TO SWEEP IT FROM AN UPSLOPE

Step 1

Match the slope
Take a wide stance, then shift most of your weight to your right foot. As you do, tilt your body away from the target so that your shoulders, hips and knees match the slope you're standing on.

Step 2

Short backswing
Make a ¾ backswing, keeping your weight on your downhill foot. Any swing longer than this may result in a loss of balance and poor contact.

Step 3

Follow the slope
Swing down with your arms—you won't be able to shift your weight because gravity is pulling you back down the hill. Swing up the slope and take just a bit of grass—if you take a divot you won't reach the green.

IMPORTANT!
Notice how the right hip points to the right of the target. That's gravity holding it back, which is why your arms must do most of the work.

KEY MOVE

Tilt to match the slope.

Stop your hands at shoulder height.

43

Swing up—not into—the slope.

SHOT

15 Approach Shot From a Downslope

The "down-and-through" move that makes this lie easy is good for your regular full swing, too

44

CLUB CHOICE

- A downhill lie subtracts loft from your club.
- Swing one club less—it'll give you the same distance but with a softer trajectory.
- If you need anything longer than a 4-iron or 7-wood from this lie, play a lay-up shot instead.

LOW BLOW

- Since you're swinging down the slope, make a lower follow-through with all of your weight on your left foot.

TURN & BURN

- You need a sharp downswing to get down to the ball from this lie, but don't forget to turn your hips.

SHOT RECIPE	
CLUB	One less than the distance
AIM	At target
STANCE	Shoulders tilted with slope
BALL POSITION	Center
SWING	Full back to a low finish
FEEL	Swing down the slope

The Situation

You smiled on the tee box when you saw that the hole you're playing ran downhill. The slope added an extra 15 yards to your drive. Standing in the fairway, however, you're not so happy—your lie is tilted just enough toward the target to give you fits. You don't feel very comfortable over the ball when your left foot is lower than your right.

The Solution

Since the slope you're on isn't too severe (if it is, consult Shot 17), you only need to fine-tune your setup and swing. That being said, don't take these alterations casually, otherwise you'll hit a low screamer that won't get to the green.

DIFFICULTY LEVEL

0   1   2   3 ▲ 4   5

If you have trouble properly hitting down on the ball from level lies (or you rarely take divots), you'll hit a lot of low liners from this lie.

HOW TO KNOCK IT ON FROM A DOWNSLOPE

First, set your body parallel with the slope. Once you achieve that, do the same with your swing. *Here's how:*

Step 1: Match your body to the slope

You can do this one of three ways:

- Take your address with the ball in the middle of your stance and raise your right foot. Why? To force your upper body to tilt to the left like it should.

- With both feet on the ground, tip your upper body to the left so that your shoulders match the slope. To check, lay your club across your chest and make sure the shaft tilts with the hill.

- To know for certain that you nailed your posture, line up your club with the buttons on your shirt. If the shaft points at the ball, you're solid.

KEY MOVE

Step 2

Take the club back along the slope. Since the ground behind the ball is higher than the ground in front of the ball, your backswing will be steeper than what you're used to.

Step 3

Swing down the slope while turning your hips so that they're open to the target at impact. If you come down steep without pivoting your lower body, you'll jam the club into the ground.

SHOT 16 Approach From a Severe Upslope

If you like to hit high draws, this is your lie

The Situation
The ball is sitting up and you have 170 yards to the green. The only problem is that the ball is resting on a severe upslope. When you go to take your stance, your left foot is several inches higher than your right.

The Solution
You're better off being here than the situation on the opposite page. From this lie, you're allowed to hang back on your right side. Normally, this produces a block. Here, it gives you a nice, soft draw with plenty of punch.

You can see how an upslope affects the loft of your clubface. You may need to drop down two clubs to produce the right distance, and since the ball is forward in your stance, there's more time for the face to close. What you end up with is a high draw.

DIFFICULTY LEVEL

0	1	2	3	4	5

If your normal move is to hang back on your right side and hit blocks or hooks, then this lie is *your* lie.

POSTURE
- Set your shoulders parallel with the slope and play the ball just slightly forward of center.
- Make sure that the top button on your shirt is behind the ball at adddres.
- If you correctly swing up the hill, your top shirt button will be behind the ball at impact, too.

Make a full shoulder turn going back to encourage a sweeping through-swing that travels up the hill.

KEY MOVE

HANG & HOLD
- Hang back on your right side until the momentum of your swing pulls you into your finish.
- Power this swing with mostly your arms, and keep your right shoulder behind the ball at impact.

SHOT RECIPE	
CLUB	One more than the distance
AIM	Slightly right of target
STANCE	Shoulders tilted with slope
BALL POSITION	One ball forward of center
SWING	Full back to a high finish
FEEL	Like you're hanging back

1. STEADY HEAD
- Try to keep your head as steady as possible and stay down on the shot.

2. MAKE IT STEEP
- Swing the club from a very high position in your backswing to a very low position in front of the ball.

3. STAY FLEXED
- Keep your right knee flexed. The moment it straightens is the moment you lose all chances of solid contact.

4. SET A BASE
- Pull your right foot back 6 inches—it will improve your balance, especially in your follow-through and finish.

5. LEAN FORWARD
- Keep the ball in the center, get your knees leaning toward the target and anchor your weight over your downhill foot.

SHOT

17
Approach From a Severe Downslope

5 keys make this shot easier than it looks

The Situation
The ball has hung up on a steep downslope. When you take your stance, your left foot is *waaay* below your right. Although you have difficulty keeping your balance, you want to play a full shot because you're only a mid-iron away from the green.

The Solution
Follow the 5 keys here and you'll be in business. Before you swing, however, aim five to 10 yards to the right (this lie causes the ball to go left) and take at least one extra club (the ball won't go as far since you won't be able to take your full cut).

47

DIFFICULTY LEVEL

| 0 | 1 | 2 | 3 | 4 | 5 |

If you don't nail all 5 moves, you won't get this shot on.

SHOT RECIPE	
CLUB	One more than distance
AIM	Right of target
STANCE	Right foot pulled back
BALL POSITION	Standard
SWING	Three-quarter swing
FEEL	Swing from high to very low

SHOT 18

Upslope and Ball Above Feet

You have two draw factors at work—this one's gonna hook

The Situation
The good news is that your slice off the tee stayed in bounds. The bad news is that on your next swing you're forced to take a stance on a steep upslope with the ball above your feet.

The Problem
When facing combination lies like this, the first step is to judge which slope is the dominant factor. Is the ball severely above your feet, or is it the upslope that's got you worried? In this situation, you're dealing with two factors that typically result in a draw. The end result is that they'll combine and produce a hard right-to-left shot.

How to Handle It
Play out to the right to accommodate the hook. That's the easy part. The second step is to match your body to the slope. Most golfers only think about their shoulders when adjusting to slopes. Your hips are just as critical. Copy the positions below to guarantee crisp contact and a controlled ballflight from a very tight spot.

DIFFICULTY LEVEL

0   1   2   3   4   5

The only thing working in your favor is that the hill will add loft to your shot, but make no mistake: this is a challenge.

ADJUST FOR THE UPSLOPE
- Tilt your left hip up (while simultaneously dropping your right hip down).
- Your body will follow your hips.
- This allows you to swing up the hill so you don't stick your club in the ground.

ADJUST FOR BALL ABOVE FEET
- Tuck your hips under your body (toward the ball). This creates the taller posture you need since the ball is closer to you.
- It also allows you to swing more around your body so you don't catch the shot fat.

Set your body to the slope using your hips. Your shoulders and swing will follow.

SHOT RECIPE	
CLUB	Two clubs more than yardage
AIM	10 yards right of target
STANCE	Hips tilted to slope and tucked
BALL POSITION	Toward left foot
SWING	Full back to 3/4 finish
FEEL	Your swing follows your hips

SHOT

19

Downslope and Ball Below Feet

Use hip power to beat the most difficult uneven lie in the game

The Situation

You're off the fairway but within striking distance of the green. When you set up on a straight line to the flag, however, the ball is below your feet and your left foot is below your right. Is this even legal?

The Solution

There are a thousand lies easier than this. Even club selection is a headache. The downslope suggests you use less club because of the de-lofting effect of the hill. Experience, however, tells you that you need more club since the ball usually fades when it sits below your feet. The trick is to determine which factor will have a greater influence on your ballflight. In other words, take an educated guess.

How to Hit It

Like you read on the opposite page, the secret to producing crisp contact on a sidehill is to adjust to the slope and lie using your hips, not your shoulders. Copy the positions at right.

DIFFICULTY LEVEL

| 0 | 1 | 2 | 3 | 4 | 5 |

Shank alert! In addition to demanding serious changes to your setup, this lie brings the hosel on your club very much into play.

SET YOUR HIPS

- Since the ball is below your feet, thrust your hips back so you can bend over more and get the club all the way down to the ball.
- In addition to pulling your hips back, tilt your right hip up so that your beltline matches the slope.
- Feel how your hips set you up to swing steep and from the inside.

49

SHOT RECIPE

CLUB	Variable
AIM	Slightly to the left
STANCE	Weight on left foot
BALL POSITION	Toward left foot
SWING	At 60% power
FEEL	Let the club release after impact

SHOT

20

How to Plan a Downhill Approach

You've got to know the actual distance of your shot, not just the yardage to the green

The Situation

You're in the fairway roughly 140 yards from the pin. Your lie is good. The only trouble is that the green sits below your spot in the fairway. Common sense tells you that you're going to get more out of your 8-iron than its usual 140 yards, but you're not sure exactly how much. You're not even sure if you need to club down.

The Solution

The best thing you can do in this situation is to follow a well-accepted general rule: Take one club less for each 30-foot drop in elevation. For example, to hit a downhill approach to a green that sits 60 feet below your lie, take two full clubs less. To really nail your club and shot selection, however, follow the steps at right.

DIFFICULTY LEVEL

| 0 | 1 | 2 | 3 | 4 | 5 |

You actually have an advantage here because the ball will come in steep and stop quickly on the green.

KEY MOVE

1: CHECK THE DROP

- Eyeball how far the green sits below you and take one less club for every 30 feet of drop.
- If you don't know what 30 feet of drop looks like, check the Extra Lesson at far right.

Take one less club for every 30-foot drop in elevation.

2: CHECK THE PIN

- Is it front, middle or back? For a front pin, you'd rather be a little long than short, and vice versa for a back pin.
- Remember that the ball will be coming in at a steeper angle, meaning it will stop quickly once it hits the green.

50

If you're unsure about the club you should use, opt for the longer one and use a 3/4-swing.

3: CHECK YOUR EGO

- Before you make a full swing with a shorter club, consider going after the ball with a longer club and a three-quarter backswing.
- The longer club gives you a greater margin for error in that you don't have to catch the ball perfectly on the sweet spot, whereas with the shorter club you have to absolutely *pure* it (and how many times do you do that?).

SHOT RECIPE

CLUB	1 less for every 30 feet of drop
AIM	At target
STANCE	Standard
BALL POSITION	Standard
SWING	Full (shorter club); ¾ (longer)
FEEL	Know your *actual* distance

How to Eyeball the Right Drop In Elevation

"Stack flagsticks" to get the true yardage to the pin

The old rule of "1 less club for every 30 feet of elevation change" holds true, but do you really know what 30 feet of elevation change looks like? Not many do, so forget about elevation drops. What you're really after is the true distance to the flag, and here's how to get it.

Look at the flagstick and calculate how many of them you'd have to stack up on top of each other until the top one was even with your ball (or, if you're below the flag, how many flagsticks would make your ball even with the hole). Take this number and multiply it by eight (roughly the height of a flagstick in feet), and then take that total and divide it by three to give you a number in yards. Subtract that number from the listed yardage to a green that's below you (or add it to the listed yardage to a green that's above you) to discover the true distance. Make your club selection based on that yardage like you would from a level approach.

51

DO THE MATH

LISTED YARDAGE: 150 YARDS
Flags stacked: 3
Drop in feet (3 x 8 feet): 24 feet
Drop in yards (24 / 3): 8 yards
Adjustment: 150 – 8
ACTUAL YARDAGE: 142 YARDS

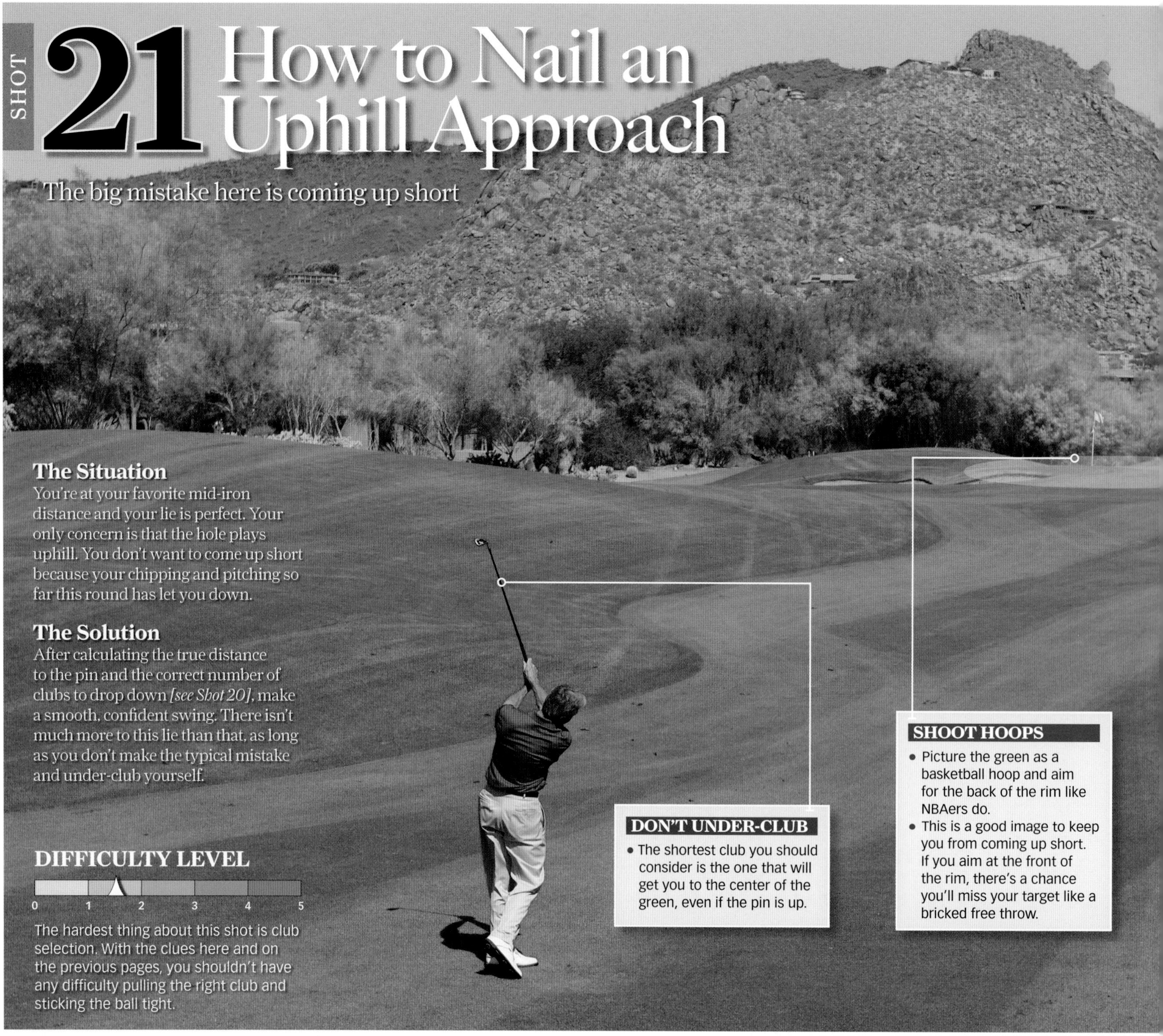

SHOT

21 How to Nail an Uphill Approach

The big mistake here is coming up short

52

The Situation

You're at your favorite mid-iron distance and your lie is perfect. Your only concern is that the hole plays uphill. You don't want to come up short because your chipping and pitching so far this round has let you down.

The Solution

After calculating the true distance to the pin and the correct number of clubs to drop down *[see Shot 20]*, make a smooth, confident swing. There isn't much more to this lie than that, as long as you don't make the typical mistake and under-club yourself.

DIFFICULTY LEVEL

| 0 | 1 | 2 | 3 | 4 | 5 |

The hardest thing about this shot is club selection. With the clues here and on the previous pages, you shouldn't have any difficulty pulling the right club and sticking the ball tight.

DON'T UNDER-CLUB

- The shortest club you should consider is the one that will get you to the center of the green, even if the pin is up.

SHOOT HOOPS

- Picture the green as a basketball hoop and aim for the back of the rim like NBAers do.
- This is a good image to keep you from coming up short. If you aim at the front of the rim, there's a chance you'll miss your target like a bricked free throw.

✓ CHECK!

Look at what the flag is doing. There might be wind above you that you can't detect because you're in a low spot.

HOW TO HIT AN UPHILL GREEN

If your club selection is correct, a solid swing will get you home. If you need to think about something, **focus on making contact with the *bottom* of the ball.** The worst thing you can do here is fall back and scoop the ball into the air. Copy these positions:

1 Make contact with the bottom of the ball (that means digging up turf).
2 Load your weight over your left foot.
3 Head even with the ball.
4 Shaft and left arm form a straight line.

KEY MOVE

Don't Do This...

Just because the green is up a hill doesn't mean you need to help the ball into the air. Scoopy impact here means your next shot will be a tough 30-yard pitch.

Do This...

Play the ball in the center of your stance and lean the shaft toward the target (set your hands on the inside of your left thigh). Get a sense for what this position feels like and try to re-create it at impact.

SHOT RECIPE

CLUB	1 more for every 30' of rise
AIM	At target
STANCE	Standard
BALL POSITION	Standard
SWING	Full back to full finish
FEEL	Hit the bottom of the ball

EXTRA LESSONS

Check for False Fronts

How to keep from falling short because of an architect's trick

Experience tells you that good course management is as important to low scores as anything. That includes identifying the optical illusions that architects create to lure you into making mistakes.

One of the most dangerous lures is the false front. Picture a hill-top green. All you want to do is carry the front of the plateau, right? Not necessarily. **There are often a few yards of fairway—sometimes *several* yards of fairway—between the top of the hill and the green. This is called a false front. When you come to a green that might have one (you won't be able to see it because you're so far below it), trust the yardage you figured to the hole.** Many modern courses color-code their flags to indicate hole location. Take that into account, and play to the number you calculated, not to what you think you see.

53

SHOT

22 Blast From a Fairway Divot

Beat a bad break with a good setup.
Then go find the guy who didn't fill it.

The Situation
Your ball has come to rest in the back of a divot in the fairway, leaving the bottom of the ball below the lead edge of your clubface. Unless you make some adjustments, you'll catch this shot thin.

The Solution
Take one less club than for a normal lie and follow the steps at right.

LOW RIDER

- When the ball is in a divot, its bottom lies below the level of the grass—and the bottom of your clubhead.
- You'll need a steeper-than-normal downswing to get down to the ball and guard against skulling it down the fairway.

GET DIRTY

- When you're finished with this shot, the back of the divot you were in should be deeper than the front. That means you properly hit down on the ball. Try and create an explosion of dirt.

DIFFICULTY LEVEL

0	1	2	3	4	5

If you have trouble hitting down on the ball from normal lies, then this one might give you some fits.

54

HOW TO BEAT A BALL IN A DIVOT

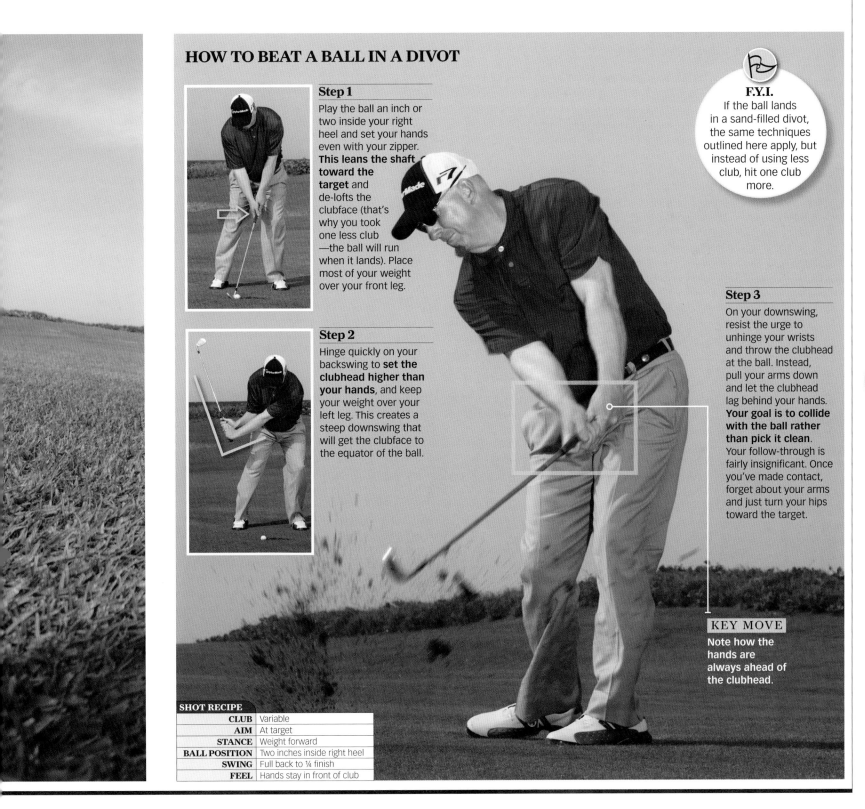

Step 1

Play the ball an inch or two inside your right heel and set your hands even with your zipper. **This leans the shaft toward the target** and de-lofts the clubface (that's why you took one less club —the ball will run when it lands). Place most of your weight over your front leg.

Step 2

Hinge quickly on your backswing to **set the clubhead higher than your hands**, and keep your weight over your left leg. This creates a steep downswing that will get the clubface to the equator of the ball.

F.Y.I.

If the ball lands in a sand-filled divot, the same techniques outlined here apply, but instead of using less club, hit one club more.

Step 3

On your downswing, resist the urge to unhinge your wrists and throw the clubhead at the ball. Instead, pull your arms down and let the clubhead lag behind your hands. **Your goal is to collide with the ball rather than pick it clean.** Your follow-through is fairly insignificant. Once you've made contact, forget about your arms and just turn your hips toward the target.

KEY MOVE

Note how the hands are always ahead of the clubhead.

SHOT RECIPE	
CLUB	Variable
AIM	At target
STANCE	Weight forward
BALL POSITION	Two inches inside right heel
SWING	Full back to ¼ finish
FEEL	Hands stay in front of club

55

SHOTS

23-25

How to Hit Partial Wedge Shots

Control the length of your swing with the image of a clock's face and hit the ball dead on the money from any distance

CHECK!
Download your personalized Distance-Control System card at **www.golf.com/dcs** and start knocking it stiff from short range.

YARD MAN

- Once you know how far you hit your PW with a full swing, hitting exact distances under 100 yards is easy.
- Shorten your swing with your PW, SW and GW to generate specific distances using the simple image of a clock.

The Situation

You have a good lie in the fairway roughly 70 yards from the green. Tour players drool at the chance to hit from this area. You, on the other hand, are dripping with fear. Unless you can make a full swing (which you can't do here because a full swing with your shortest club gives you 80 yards), you have difficulty producing the correct distance for your lie. Even when you try to make half, three-quarter and other partial swings, the ball ends up miles from the flagstick.

The Solution

The problem with partial swings is that it's difficult to tell what 1/2- and 3/4-swings feel like. But they're an absolute necessity. Instead of trying to feel your way around your swing, use the image of a clock to stop your swing at specific lengths and generate numerous and exact distances with each of your wedges.

DIFFICULTY LEVEL

| 0 | 1 | 2 | 3 | 4 | 5 |

This is an easy technique to learn. Once you have it down, it will pay extremely positive dividends in your scoring.

SHOT RECIPE	
CLUB	SW, GW or PW
AIM	At target
STANCE	Standard
BALL POSITION	Standard
SWING	Match swing to yardage
FEEL	You're swinging in a clock

How to Do It

Grab your pitching wedge and hit balls out onto the practice range with your full swing. As you make these swings, **picture a clock's face tilted on the same plane as your swing** (with your chest at the center of the face). On a full swing with your pitching wedge, your hands swing back to 10 o'clock in your backswing and 12 o'clock in your finish.

Determine the distance you get with your good 10-to-12 pitching-wedge swings. Then, change the times to generate shorter distances. After practicing these swings, apply the clock image to swings with your gap and sand wedges. By using the simple image of a clock face, you can build an inventory of wedge swings that hit the ball to every yardage within 100 yards.

Dial It In

Use the table below (developed by Top 100 Teacher Ted Sheftic) to generate every distance from 110 yards all the way down to 20 yards (at 10-yard increments). **If you hit your full pitching wedge farther or shorter than the 110-yard example outlined here, visit golf.com/dcs and download the swing table that matches the distance you typically generate with a full pitching wedge.** Use it to hit it tight from 100 yards and in every time.

FULL PW DISTANCE: 110 YARDS

Distance	Club	Swing
110	PW	10 to 12
100	PW	9 to 12
90	GW	10 to 12
80	GW	9 to 12
70	GW (SW)	9 to 2 (11 to 12)
60	SW	10 to 12
50	SW	9 to 12
40	SW	9 to 2
30	SW	8 to 3
20	SW	8 to 4

100 YARDS — **PITCHING**

If your full pitching wedge flies 110 yards and you need to hit the ball 100 yards...
Swing your pitching wedge from 9 o'clock to 12 o'clock.

80 YARDS — **GAP**

If your full pitching wedge flies 110 yards and you need to hit the ball 80 yards...
Swing your gap wedge from 9 o'clock to 2 o'clock.

60 YARDS — **SAND**

If your full pitching wedge flies 110 yards and you need to hit the ball 60 yards...
Swing your sand wedge from 10 o'clock to 12 o'clock.

57

SHOT

26

From In-Between Distances

Is it a 6-iron or a 7-iron? Here's how to make the right choice and stiff it when you're torn between two clubs.

The Situation
You hit a good drive to the center of the fairway, but as you step off the yardage to the green you discover that you're 5 yards farther than what you can comfortably hit your 7-iron and 5 yards shorter of what you usually get from a good swing with your 6-iron.

The Solution
Taking yards off or adding yards to the distance you hit each iron in your bag is an important skill. If you don't have it, then you'll get the ball close to the pin only when it sits at 8 distinct distances (one for each iron you carry), and the chances of that happening aren't very good. Check the clues at right to help you decide between a hard shot with a shorter iron or a soft shot with a longer one, then consult the sequences at far right for how to pull off each one.

DIFFICULTY LEVEL

| 0 | 1 | 2 | 3 | 4 | 5 |

The fact that you're at an in-between distance shouldn't stop you from hitting the green. Ever.

HIT THE LONGER CLUB IF...
- The hole plays uphill.
- The wind is in your face.
- There's trouble short.
  Also, make sure the distance you're sitting at is to the *pin*, not the center of the green. If you only know the distance to the center, play the longer club if the pin is middle or back.

SHOT RECIPE	
CLUB	Variable
AIM	At target
STANCE	Standard
BALL POSITION	Back (shorter); forward (long)
SWING	Full (shorter iron); ¾ (longer)
FEEL	Same pace for both shots

58

If you're a high-handicapper, always play the longer club. It'll give you a softer trajectory and you won't feel like you have to kill it.

HIT THE SHORTER CLUB IF...

- The hole plays downhill.
- The wind is at your back.
- There's trouble long.
  If you only know the distance to the center, play the shorter club if the pin is in the front.

KEY MOVE

When hitting a longer club, choke up an inch or two on the handle. This shortens the club and makes it easier to control.

HOW TO ADD 5 YARDS TO AN IRON

Step 1
Play the ball just back of center and lean the shaft forward. This de-lofts the clubface, turning your 7-iron, for example, into a 6.5-iron.

Step 2
Make a full backswing. From the top, feel like you're going to pinch the ball between the clubface and the grass, not pick it off the turf.

Step 3
Accelerate to a full finish, with everything (hips, shoulders, head) facing the target and your weight over your left foot.

59

HOW TO SUBTRACT 5 YARDS FROM AN IRON

Step 1
Play the ball forward, just off your left heel, and set your hands directly above the ball.

Step 2
Make a ¾-backswing (stop your swing when you feel your hands reach shoulder height).

Step 3
Without changing speeds, swing to a ¾-finish (make sure you turn fully toward the target).

SHOT 27

Put a Low Draw In Your Bag

This scrambling tool can also give you 10 more yards

What It Is
A lower-than-normal shot that curves from right-to-left and runs hard once it lands.

When to Use It
The situation pictured here is a good example: you missed the fairway left but a tree is on a direct line to the pin. Hitting over the tree won't give you enough yardage to the green and you don't want to waste a shot playing straight back to the fairway

How to Hit It
This isn't a hard shot to learn: With a few setup adjustments, you can draw the ball with your normal swing.

DIFFICULTY LEVEL

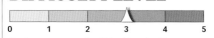

| 0 | 1 | 2 | 3 | 4 | 5 |

As long as you don't hold onto the clubface or chicken-wing the shot, you'll get the results you want every time.

60

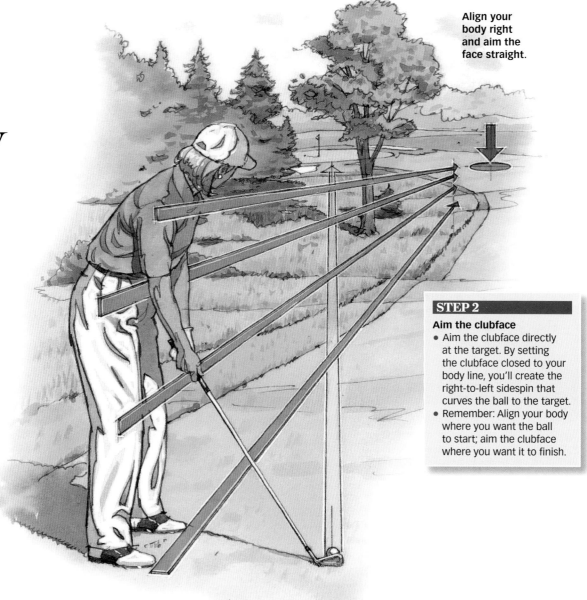

Align your body right and aim the face straight.

STEP 2

Aim the clubface
- Aim the clubface directly at the target. By setting the clubface closed to your body line, you'll create the right-to-left sidespin that curves the ball to the target.
- Remember: Align your body where you want the ball to start; aim the clubface where you want it to finish.

STEP 1

Aim your body at the target
- Body alignment determines the ball's initial direction.
- Pick a spot right of the target (say, the right edge of the fairway) and align your feet, knees, hips and shoulders to that point. This allows for the shot's curve.

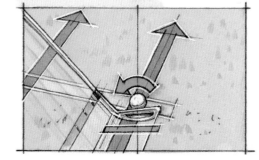

Setting the face closed to your body line and moving the club along your body line will produce right-to-left sidespin.

SHOT
29
High Fade
Approach

Make this your bread-and-butter shot to front-right pins

The Situation
You have obstacles (likely trees) on the right that you need curve the ball around, or you're attacking a front-right pin position.

The Solution
Hit a high fade shot that curves from left-to-right around those trees and lands softly on the green. The best part is that you probably hit this shot frequently without even trying.

SHOT RECIPE	
CLUB	5-iron at most
AIM	Clubface at arget
STANCE	Left of target
BALL POSITION	Between center and left heel
SWING	At full speed
FEEL	You're holding the face open

63

HOW TO HIT A HIGH FADE

Step 1
Take any iron and make sure the clubface is open at least 5 degrees (making your 5-iron, for example, look like your 6-iron). Aim the clubface at the target and aim your body toward the line on which you want to the ball to start (about 5 to 10 yards left of the target).

Step 2
Position the ball forward of center for this shot, about halfway between the middle of your stance and your left heel.

Step 3
When you swing, focus on rotating your body a little faster than you normally would and keep the back of your left hand facing the target at impact. Don't roll your forearms over because you want to hit the ball with an open clubface.

DIFFICULTY LEVEL

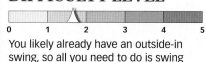

0   1   2   3   4   5

You likely already have an outside-in swing, so all you need to do is swing outside-in a little faster.

30 Low Fade Approach

Use it to fly the ball under and around obstacles and still hit the green

What It Is

A shot the curves from left to right and flies on a lower-than-normal trajectory.

When to Use It

When you need to carve the ball into a headwind to a far-right hole location or escape some low-hanging tree limbs.

How to Hit It

Buyer beware—a low fade isn't the easiest shot to create under normal conditions as a fade usually wants to climb quickly. But it can be a great weapon when the situation calls for it. To execute this shot, aim your body left (where you want the ball to start) and point the clubface at the target (where you want the ball to finish). Play the ball an inch or two farther back in your stance than normal, with your weight favoring your left foot. This combination starts the shot on a low trajectory. Make no more than a three-quarter backswing and focus on keeping the toe of the clubhead from passing the heel until after impact. This will keep the face slightly open and give you the left-to-right spin you need to fade this shot.

DIFFICULTY LEVEL

0	1	2	3	4	5

This is the toughest curve to pull off, since a fade normally wants to climb. Think of it as a punch hit with an open clubafce.

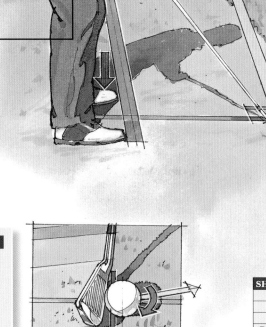

CLUB CHOICES

- For best results use a 5-, 6-, or 7-iron.
- These clubs have enough loft to get the ball airborne even with the ball back in your stance, but not so much loft that the backspin generated will override the sidespin needed to curve the shot from left-to-right.

FADE FACTORS

- Align your body left of target.
- Aim the clubface at the target.

LOW FACTORS

- Position the ball back in your stance.
- Shift your weight so that it favors your front foot.

KEY MOVE

AVOID A CROSS

- The last thing you want here is a low hook. Hold the face open through impact to help the ball travel on a left-to-right

SHOT RECIPE

CLUB	Any iron (mid-irons preferred)
AIM	Clubface at target
STANCE	Left of target
BALL POSITION	Between center and right foot
SWING	3/4 back to 3/4 finish
FEEL	You're holding the face open

SHOT **31** How to Attack a Back Pin

Whether you're hitting to a par-3 green or in the fairway plotting your approach, heed the Top 100's advice for getting all the way back to the flag

The Situation

You're on the tee of a 125-yard par 3 (or have 125 yards left from the fairway). The pin is cut in the middle of the third tier on a green that slopes back to front. A stiff 20-mph wind is in your face.

The Solution

Match your preferred style of play with the shot that leaves you with the best percentage to get close. *[For more on knockdown shots, see page 66.]*

Wind direction

65

SHOT RECIPE

CLUB	Variable
AIM	Variable
STANCE	Variable
BALL POSITION	Variable
SWING	Variable
FEEL	Confidence in your selection

DIFFICULTY LEVEL

| 0 | 1 | 2 | 3 | 4 | 5 |

Making the right decision here is as easy as accurately judging your strengths and weaknesses.

IF YOU'RE AN AGGRESSIVE PLAYER...

Hit a knockdown to the pin.

Club selection: If the card says the hole is 125 yards and the pin is back, figure you have 135 to the hole. The general rule for playing into the wind is one more club for every 10 mph. So if you normally hit a 9-iron from 135 yards, you should drop down to a 7-iron here. But since you're going to play a knockdown, drop down one more club to a 6-iron.

Swing tip: Trust that you have enough club and make a three-quarter swing back and through.

Target: Aim at the middle of the second tier. Your knockdown shot should skip forward to the third tier before it grabs.

IF YOU TEND TO SLICE OR HOOK YOUR IRONS...

Play a low shot to the middle tier, because you need to keep spin to a minimum, and low shots spin less. Plus, if you hit your normal shot you'll end up short.

Club selection: Plus two clubs for the wind.

Swing tip: You don't need a pure knockdown—just something slightly lower to keep the ball under the wind. Think of hitting a long chip—play the ball back of center and focus on squaring the clubface with your body, not your hands. That means rotating your hips and shoulders to the left of your target from the top of your backswing to well past impact.

Target: Center of the green.

NOT CONFIDENT WITH THE KNOCKDOWN SHOT...

Hit a regular full-swing shot to the middle tier.

Club selection: Drop down two clubs for the wind and make your normal swing. If you pure it you might reach the back tier. If you don't, you'll still have an excellent chance for a two-putt par.

Swing tip: Forget the wind and make a relaxed swing. Don't try to "power" the ball or juice up your tempo, because even if you pure it you'll just create more backspin and the ball will fly higher (and shorter) into the wind.

Target: Even though you're planning to land your ball on the middle tier of the green, you should still aim for the top of the pin.

SHOT

32 Knock It Low Into the Wind

Even a stiff breeze is no match for this low-boring bullet

The Situation
You're in the fairway, mid-iron distance to the pin, with a stiff breeze in your face.

The Solution
You might think about making your normal swing with an extra club or two, but the normal loft of even a 5-iron might be too high (the wind will

ADDRESS
- Play the ball back in your stance—directly off the toes of your right foot.
- Forward press your hands so that the shaft leans toward the target.
- If your normal grip pressure is a "7" on a 1-to-10 scale, make it a "9" here.

BACKSWING
- Make a shorter, more compact backswing (notice how this doesn't mean restricting your shoulder and hip turn).
- Feel like your left arm is connected to your chest.

F.Y.I.
Some players use the knockdown when they're hitting with the wind at their back so the breeze can't carry the shot too far.

66

quickly stop any lofted shot in its tracks). Better golfers play the knockdown shot, a controlled, low-flying bullet that stays below the wind and travels straight at the target. The knockdown also is a good play when you have to keep the ball low under a tree or you need to pitch the ball and there's plenty of room between you and the pin.

How to Knock It Into the Wind

Take two extra clubs (a 6-iron if you're at your 8-iron distance) and follow the steps below. The ball won't spin much, but you can still play the full distance to your target because the wind will stop the ball quickly once it hits.

DIFFICULTY LEVEL

Anytime you have to control swing length it becomes easy to lose your natural rhythm and tempo. On the range, practice keeping the same speed both back and through.

KEY MOVE

DOWNSWING
- Make an aggressive move from the top of your backswing.
- Try to keep your left arm firm. Use your body to move your straight left arm from a horizontal position *[photo, left]* to a vertical position at impact. Don't go soft on this shot!

FINISH
- Like you did with your backswing, abbreviate your finish, but make sure that your head, chest, hips and knees are facing the target, just like they do in your everyday full swing.
- The ball will come out low and hot—it will rise a little but settle quickly once it hits the turf.

SHOT RECIPE	
CLUB	Two more than the distance
AIM	At target
STANCE	Standard
BALL POSITION	Off right foot
SWING	Compact back and through
FEEL	Keep your left arm strong

67

33 Approach With a Crosswind

Whether you fight it or ride it, here's all you need to get it close

POLL

With a left-to-right wind, the Top 100 Teachers say...
45%—Play your fade and ride the wind.
22%—Fight the wind and play a draw.
19%—Hit into the wind and let it blow your ball back.
14%—Other (long-iron, hybrids, low shots).

68

SHOT RECIPE

CLUB	Variable
AIM	Left (fade); straight (draw)
STANCE	Standard
BALL POSITION	Forward (fade); back (draw)
SWING	Standard
FEEL	Forearm roll for a draw

DIFFICULTY LEVEL

0 1 2 3 ▲ 4 5

These are standard draws and fades, but if you misjudge the strength of the wind or double-cross yourself (hit a fade instead of a draw), you're in some deep trouble.

The Situation

You have a good lie in the fairway (or you're on the tee of a par 3) with your favorite mid-iron in your hands, and you're looking to pounce on this birdie opportunity. Unfortunately, there's a 20-mph wind blowing from left-to-right across the fairway. You don't know whether to aim left of your desired target and let the ball ride the wind in, or play straight and hold the ball against the breeze with a draw or hook.

The Solution

Either play is correct. The best one for you depends on your ability and style of play.

RIDE IT

In a left-to-right crosswind, ride the breeze with a fade.
- Aim left of the flagstick.
- Open your clubface (rotate to the right) at address.
- Don't roll your left forearm through impact.

Rotate the face open at ½-hour increments to generate the correct amount of fade.

12:30
10-yd fade

1:00
20-yd fade

FIGHT IT

In a left-to-right crosswind, fight the breeze with a draw.
- Aim at the flagstick (or your desired landing spot).
- Close your clubface (rotate to the left) at address.
- Roll your left forearm to the left through impact.

Rotate the face closed at ½-hour increments to generate the correct amount of draw.

11:30
10-mph wind

11:00
20-mph wind

IF YOU CAN WORK THE BALL...

...Play a hold-up draw

Stand slightly farther from the ball and position it two balls' widths back of where you normally play it with the club in your hands. Take dead aim at your target and close the face to match the severity of the wind *[see guide on opposite page]*.

As you swing through impact, make an extra effort to roll your left forearm so that its underside points to the sky in your release *[photo, below left]*. You know you've done it right if the toe of the clubhead points left of your target in your follow-through *[photo, below right]*.

KEY MOVE

IF YOU'RE A FADER...

...Ride the wind

Stand closer to the ball and position it one ball's width forward of where you normally play it with the club in your hands. Aim 10 yards left of your target for, say, a 10-mph wind and 20 yards left for a 20-mph wind. Then, open the face to match the breeze *[see guide on opposite page]*. Cut the amount of slice you need in half since the wind will add to the curve (i.e., open the face for a 10-yard fade if you're aimed 20 yards left of the target.

As you swing through impact, feel like the underside of your right forearm is pointing up more than it points down the line *[photo, below left]*. You know you've done it right if the toe of the clubhead points skyward as you

KEY MOVE

SHOT

34 Downwind Approach

Swing easy and let the breeze do the rest

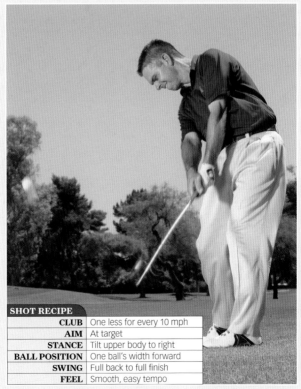

The Situation

You're facing a mid-iron approach from a perfect lie. There's a 20-mph breeze at your back.

The Solution

Some players like hitting knockdowns in this situation *[Shot 32]*. A much easier play is to swing a shorter club and let the wind carry the ball all the way to your target.

How to Hitch a Ride

There are 3 things you need to think about: Address and club selection, your finish position and swing speed.

SHOT RECIPE	
CLUB	One less for every 10 mph
AIM	At target
STANCE	Tilt upper body to right
BALL POSITION	One ball's width forward
SWING	Full back to full finish
FEEL	Smooth, easy tempo

1. Setup

Use one less club for every 10 mph of wind. If you don't know what 10 mph of wind feels like, toss some grass in the air. If the grass lands 10 feet in front of you, you have a 10-mph wind.

Position the ball just forward of where you play it with the club you're holding and tilt your upper body to the right. Grip the club at the end of the handle and use the lightest grip pressure that still gives you complete control of the club.

2. Finish

Focus on completing your swing with a high finish, with your hands above your head. This is a good image to help you release the club fully so the ball gets up in the air and rides the wind.

3. Swing Speed

It's easy to lose your rhythm in windy conditions, but here it's extra important that you make a smooth swing. Practice your swing with the last two fingers on your left hand off the grip. Swing hard enough to make a complete motion without the club slipping from your hands. Re-create that tempo and speed when you play your shot.

KEY MOVE

DIFFICULTY LEVEL

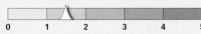

0   1   2   3   4   5

This shot is simply your everyday swing performed with less club. Consider yourself lucky to hit with a helping wind.

69

35

Long-Iron Approach

Three easy
moves make
you deadly with
your 4-iron on down

70

The Situation

You're in the fairway but a good distance—
at least 180 yards—from the green. A hybrid
or fairway wood is too much club. You need
a solid 3- or 4-iron into the green and you
don't hit these clubs solid very often.

The Solution

Most golfers struggle to hit crisp long irons
because they swing a little too steep and a
little to out-to-in. This works well with short
irons because they have more upright lie
angles. Long irons are built much flatter, so
when you swing them steeply you take a lot
of turf and make contact out toward the toe.
The secret is to shallow out your angle of
attack. *Here's how:*

SHOT RECIPE	
CLUB	Long iron
AIM	At target
STANCE	Shoulder-width
BALL POSITION	Between center and left foot
SWING	Full back to full finish
FEEL	Right shoulder down

HOW TO SMOKE YOUR 4-IRON

Step 1

Tilt your upper body to the right at address. Get the
buttons on your shirt to the right of your belt buckle.

Step 2

At the start
of your
downswing,
move your
right shoulder
toward the
ground. Feel
like gravity
is pulling it
straight down.
Don't swing
your right
shoulder out
toward the
target.

KEY MOVE

**Drop your right shoulder down
to start your downswing.**

Step 3

End your
swing with
a high finish,
with your
hands above
your head and
the clubhead
below your
hands. If
you're high
at the finish,
it means you
were low
(shallow)
through the
hitting area.

**Hands
higher than
clubhead.**

DIFFICULTY LEVEL

0   1   2   3   4   5

The longer the iron, the more difficult it is to control.
If you struggle hitting your 3-, 4- and even 5-iron, fill
out your bag with easier-to-hit hybrids.

Strike the ground on your practice swing to groove the right kind of action.

F.Y.I.
The lake guarding the island green at TPC Sawgrass swallows over 120,000 balls per year (over an average of 40,000 rounds).

Hit down on the ball to get it up.

SHOT RECIPE	
CLUB	Variable
AIM	At target
STANCE	Standard
BALL POSITION	Variable
SWING	Full back to full finish
FEEL	Pinch the ball against turf

SHOT **36**
Carry Over Water

Use this pre-shot trick to hit the ball high and keep it dry

What It Is
An approach shot that must travel its full length over a lake or other hazard.

When to Use It
In the obvious situations, as well as any time you face a pressure-packed shot.

How to Hit It
First, ignore your fears and replace them with confident thoughts. Then, use your pre-shot time to groove a swing that'll leave you close to the pin.

How to Defy The Drink
Take practice swings until you can identify the swing that fits the shot. In this case, you're looking for a crisp, downward strike. **Keep your posture steady as you swing down**, letting your left shoulder pull you through impact. Once you've felt a swing you like, step up to the ball and repeat the swing. Do it smoothly—hesitating only leaves time for negative thoughts. End with a full follow-through, making sure your belt buckle faces the target at your finish. This is a positive image that will help you correctly accelerate down and through the ball.

71

DIFFICULTY LEVEL

0	1	2	3	4	5

Flying an obstacle shouldn't be too much to handle; your goal is to always get the ball airborne.

37 Lay Up Smart on a Par 5

You're not always going to be able to go for it. Here's how to play short of the green for birdie, not bogey.

The Situation

You're playing a long par 5, and while your drive is sitting in the fairway, the green is just too far away to think about going for it in two.

The Solution

Hit a lay up short of the green. Here you have more options than on any other shot, but if you're like most golfers, you almost always choose the same one: blasting your 3-wood as far as you can. This is the reason you often walk away from a par 5 with a nasty "7" on your scorecard.

How to Lay Up Smart

Before you attempt the longest possible shot (which is the easiest to hit off line, i.e. into the rough or other trouble), consider the three questions posed here.

1. IS THE PIN CLEAR?

- If the pin is in a favorable center position with no trouble in front, go ahead and blast away with your 3-wood. Pick a precise landing spot and make a smooth, controlled swing—don't try to "kill it." You'll have an unobstructed chip to the hole.

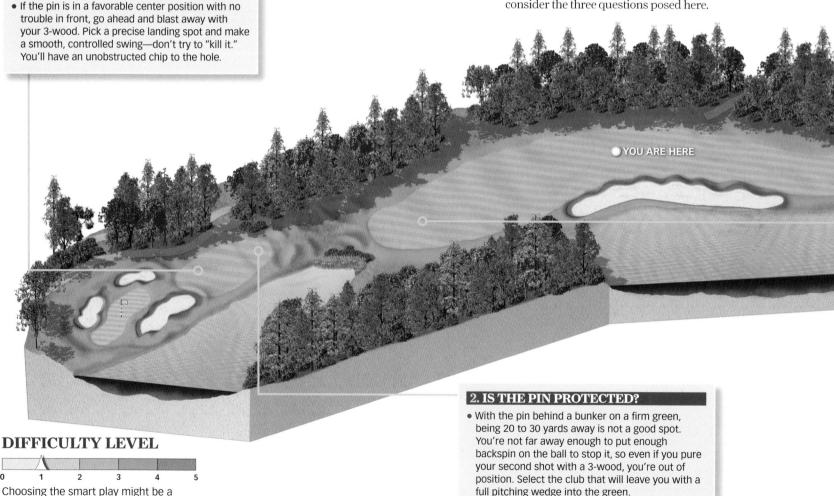

YOU ARE HERE

2. IS THE PIN PROTECTED?

- With the pin behind a bunker on a firm green, being 20 to 30 yards away is not a good spot. You're not far away enough to put enough backspin on the ball to stop it, so even if you pure your second shot with a 3-wood, you're out of position. Select the club that will leave you with a full pitching wedge into the green.

DIFFICULTY LEVEL

| 0 | 1 | 2 | 3 | 4 | 5 |

Choosing the smart play might be a challenge to your ego, but not to your mind.

72

CHECK!
Just because this is a lay-up doesn't mean you can cut corners. Make practice swings and treat it like any other shot.

LAY-UP ROUTINE

Take these steps to avoid that "mind drift" that comes on lay-up shots:
1 Play to a target, not just a yardage. Visualize a green and flagstick covering your lay-up spot.
2 Go through your pre-shot routine. Start behind the ball, take a practice swing, and treat it like any other shot.
3 Think "lay-up" from the beginning. Do it before you tee off. If you prepare yourself for a lay-up from the start, you won't be disappointed when the time comes.

KEY MOVE

3. WHAT'S YOUR FAVORITE CLUB?

● If your distance control on full-wedge shots is inconsistent, but you always hit your 8-iron 140 yards, then pick a lay-up spot 140 yards from the green. Focus on that landing area as though it were the actual green. Laying up is a numbers game, and you want to hit yours on the money.

SHOT RECIPE	
CLUB	Variable
AIM	At target
STANCE	Variable
BALL POSITION	Variable
SWING	Variable
FEEL	Treat lay-ups like regular shots

The Rules Guy

Shotmaking by the Book

"Caddie, my snorkel, please!"

Your 3-wood that was meant to land on a par-5 green in two found a water hazard fronting the green. Before you decide what to do, check the stakes around the hazard. If they're yellow, you're in a regular water hazard. You have the option of playing the ball as it lies (without penalty). If you forgot your wetsuit or have a healthy fear of water moccasins, you can take your one-stroke penalty and drop as near as possible to the spot where you played the shot that ended up in the water, or drop a ball behind the hazard keeping the point where your ball last dove in. **If you're dropping behind the hazard, you can drop as far back of it as you like, a good idea to keep in mind if you have a favorite approach distance**.

Red stakes mean you're in a lateral water hazard and the Rules are a little different. All of the options for a regular water hazard are at your disposal, but you also have the option on the side of the hazard. Imagine you hit your tee shot into a creek running along the right side of the fairway. If the creek is a lateral hazard, you could play your ball two club-lengths from where your ball last crossed the margin of the creek, or at an equidistant point from the hole on the opposite side of the creek from where the ball went in. Hey, it could give you an easier shot into the green.

73

Look through your fingers to lay an imaginary dispersion pattern (indicated by the colored circles) over different targets on the green.

SHOT 38

How to Attack a Par-3 Green

Overlay your "miss" pattern on the green to dial-in the right target

The Situation

You're on the tee of a 160-yard par 3. The pin is in the middle and the green is guarded on all sides. Past experience tells you that you shouldn't go straight at the flag, but you don't have a good feel for when and how to play safe.

The Solution

The trick to playing par 3s (as well as planning any approach shot) is to eliminate worst-case scenarios. This won't always leave you with a tap-in for birdie, but it will keep large numbers off your scorecard.

How to Do It

Make a goalpost with your fingers and peer through it to the green [photo above]. The distance between your fingers is the average mid-iron dispersion pattern for a mid-handicapped golfer. (Make the goalpoast narrower if you're a better player and wider if you're a novice or high-handicapper.) **Move the goalpost around the green until you find the spot that covers the largest area of the putting surface** (or boxes in the least number of hazards). This area may be several yards from the pin, but making the center of your goalpost your landing spot means you'll stay out of trouble and, minus a 3-putt, card par at worst.

DIFFICULTY LEVEL

| 0 | 1 | 2 | 3 | 4 | 5 |

Any golfer can learn to aim and select targets correctly, including novices and high-handicappers.

JUST RIGHT

- In this example, the best place to overlay your dispersion pattern is the front left portion of the green.
- Here, every shot out of an imaginary 100 would land safely on or near the green (and not in a hazard). Make the center of this pattern your landing point.

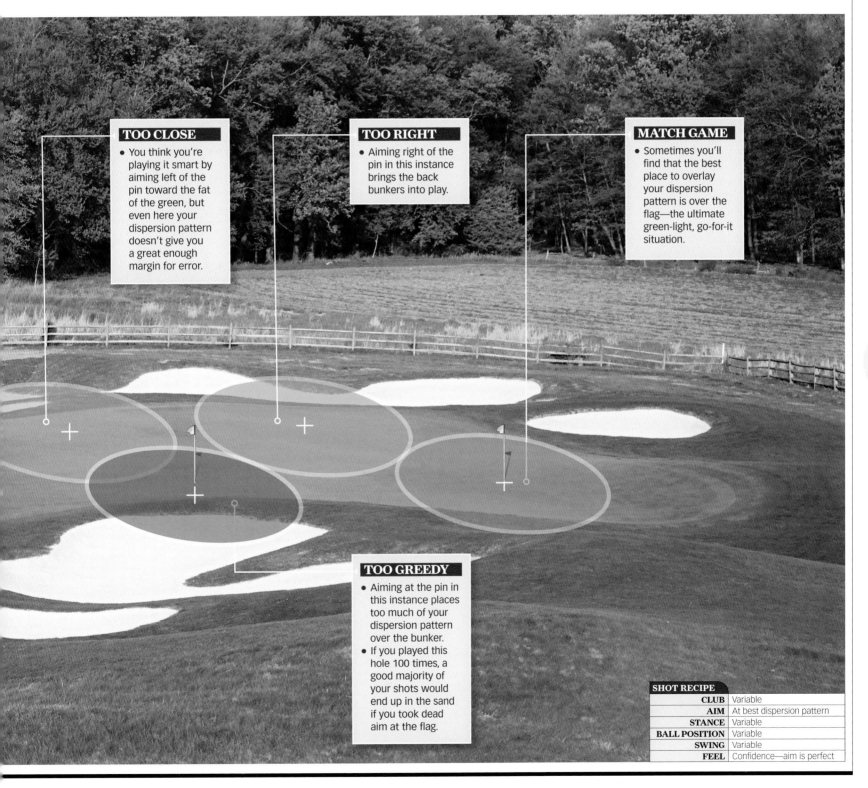

TOO CLOSE
- You think you're playing it smart by aiming left of the pin toward the fat of the green, but even here your dispersion pattern doesn't give you a great enough margin for error.

TOO RIGHT
- Aiming right of the pin in this instance brings the back bunkers into play.

MATCH GAME
- Sometimes you'll find that the best place to overlay your dispersion pattern is over the flag—the ultimate green-light, go-for-it situation.

TOO GREEDY
- Aiming at the pin in this instance places too much of your dispersion pattern over the bunker.
- If you played this hole 100 times, a good majority of your shots would end up in the sand if you took dead aim at the flag.

SHOT RECIPE	
CLUB	Variable
AIM	At best dispersion pattern
STANCE	Variable
BALL POSITION	Variable
SWING	Variable
FEEL	Confidence—aim is perfect

SHOT

39 Approach Shot From the Rough

Getting on gets tough when the grass bends away from the target

The Situation

You blocked or pushed your tee shot into the second cut of rough. When you get to the ball you're pleasantly surprised—the lie isn't that bad and you only have 140 yards left to the pin. Forget about playing a wedge back to the fairway—you're getting this baby on!

The Solution

Step 1 is to check the lie. If the grass is growing away from the target, you have serious issues to consider *[see Shot 40 if the grass is growing toward the target]*. Because the direction of the grain is opposite the direction of your swing, the grass is going to slow down your clubhead, grab the hosel and shut the clubface. Sounds tricky, but executing this shot is 90 percent setup.

DIFFICULTY LEVEL

0	1	2	3	4	5

This shot gets more difficult the longer the club you use. If you're hitting a 7-iron or less, expect very good results.

LIE CHECK

- If the grass is growing away from the target, take one more club than the distance and set up to make a sharp up-and-down swing.

STEEP ATTACK

- Stand closer to the ball and use extra wrist hinge to produce a steep downswing.
- The steeper your swing, the less time the grass has to slow down your club and/or close the face.

DON'T BRUSH

- The more you think about sweeping or brushing the ball off the rough, the more likely you'll come up short of the green. Save your flat approach for another swing.

SHOT RECIPE	
CLUB	One more than the distance
AIM	At target
STANCE	Closer to ball, open clubface
BALL POSITION	Slightly back of normal
SWING	Steep going back and through
FEEL	Thumbs at head going back

HOW TO GET IT ON WHEN YOU'RE AGAINST THE GRAIN

Step 1

Stand a little closer to the ball and play it slightly back of its normal position with the club in your hands. Standing closer will help you swing the club more up-and-down and reduce the time it spends in contact with the grass.

Open the clubface a few degrees to offset the shut-down affect of the grass and grip the club tighter than you normally do.

Step 2

When most golfers try to swing upright, they usually do it by lifting their arms without turning their shoulders. You won't get the ball all the way on with that kind of swing. Just make your regular motion but with extra wrist hinge. Try to point your thumbs at the sky as you swing the club to the top *[photo, below]*. That will give you the steepness you need to come down sharply on the ball and keep the grass from negating your speed and closing the face.

KEY MOVE

Point your thumbs at the sky early in your backswing to create a steep angle of attack.

40 From a Flyer Lie

This ball won't spin, so plan on plenty of roll

The Situation

You're in the second cut of rough, but your ball is sitting up and the grass is growing toward the target.

LESS CLUB
Use one or even two clubs less to offset the extra carry and roll you get from a flyer.

KEY MOVE

HINGE REDUX
Use the same full wrist hinge you use when the grass is growing away from the target.

The Solution

This is a shot you can get on, so check the distance and once you decide what club to swing, take the next shortest one. Wait—shorter? That's correct. Even though you're in the rough, the grass won't slow down your swing because the blades are growing in the same direction as the path your clubhead takes through impact. Moreover, the blades that get caught between the ball and your iron's sweet spot dramatically decrease the amount of backspin generated at impact, making the ball carry much farther and roll like crazy once it hits the ground.

DIFFICULTY LEVEL

```
0    1    2    3    4    5
```

Most lies in the rough are disaster situations. This one is almost too perfect. Get club and target selection right and you'll knock it on with ease.

SHOT RECIPE	
CLUB	One less than the distance
AIM	At target
STANCE	Standard
BALL POSITION	Slightly forward of normal
SWING	Steep back and through
FEEL	Carry short then let it roll

Off The Fairway

CHAPTER

4

Recovering From Trouble

Landing in the rough—or worse—shouldn't mean wasting a stroke. Here's how to not only escape, but escape and save par.

YOUR FAVORITE GOLFER on the PGA Tour hits 2 out of every 3 fairways. You're likely hitting less than that (maybe *much* less), which means that at least half of your second shots take place in the rough, the trees and, during a really bad ballstriking day, the fairway next door. Now isn't the time to panic—it's the time to fight and scramble like a cagey veteran. The fighting will require you to make some major adjustments to your swing and take on some risk, but these aren't anything you can't handle. Keep in the back of your mind that the primary key when hitting from bad lies is making sure your club strikes the ball before it strikes anything else. This chapter teaches you to master this key and turn a disaster situation into something as easy as making clean contact.

SHOT

41
Escape From Gnarly Rough

Fix your slice for straighter drives, but keep it in your pocket to save par from nasty lies

80

What It Is
An explosion shot you hit like a slice.

When to Use It
When your ball finds the really deep stuff. Call it fescue, junk—whatever. If you can't see your ball, or if the grass is higher than the top of the ferrule when you sole your club on the ground, you'll need this play. It's better than a standard hack-out with your wedge because it allows you to use a longer club and get the ball closer to the green.

How to Hit It
Remember the tee shot that got you into this horrible place? It's the one where you tried to squash a bug on a 10-foot ceiling with an ultra-steep backswing followed by a cut downswing that left a crater-sized divot on the tee box that pointed way left of your target. With a mid-iron and that ugly, steep, cut swing, you'll have no problem with this lie.

SLICE IT OUT
- The steep cut swing associated with slicing limits contact time between the clubhead and the grass, so you can get more on the shot and power it further down the fairway.
- Since your clubface is open (a natural byproduct of a cut path), the shutdown from the grass will make everything flush at contact.

SHOT RECIPE	
CLUB	Mid-iron
AIM	At target
STANCE	Shoulder-width
BALL POSITION	Center
SWING	Full back to full finish
FEEL	Steep and across

HOW TO SLICE IT FROM THE ROUGH

Step 1
Take your regular address position with any mid-iron and **make sure you're aimed at a safe spot** in the fairway, not at another trouble spot. Take care when you sole your club behind the ball—the grass your club touches might jostle the ball, giving you a penalty.

Step 2
Make a steep, full backswing. **Think about getting your hands high above your right shoulder**. To make it even steeper, swing back more with your arms and less with your body.

Step 3
Swing down sharply by pulling the club straight down and your left shoulder back. Feel like you're cutting across the ball, not swinging out toward the target. The combination of steep and across gives you're plenty of power while limiting contact with the grass.

81

Set the clubface square to your target line. Your cut swing will cause it to be open at impact, but the rough will grab hold of the hosel and quickly shut the face down, giving you a straight shot.

KEY MOVE

Do This...
From the top, come down sharply and across the line. You know you're doing it right if the clubhead moves outside your hands.

Not This...
If you come in on-plane (a goal on most swings, but not this one), your club will spend more time in contact with the grass. Your impact will feel dead and the ball won't go as far, making your next shot much longer than it could be.

DIFFICULTY LEVEL

0 1 2 3 4 5

The length of the grass is a factor, but since you're here it's likely you already have this swing grooved.

SHOT

42 Deep Rough Gouge Out

You missed the fairway. Big deal. This power play immediately gets you back in the hole.

The Situation
Your ball has come to rest in the rough. The grass isn't long *[consult shot 41 for this situation]* but it's thick, covering the ball on all sides.

The Solution
Throw any chances of hitting the green from this lie out the window. This is gouge time—a 9-iron at best. You're going to use a lot of the elements from your bunker swing, but instead of sliding your club through sand, you'll slam it steeply into the back of the ball and do it fast enough so the grass doesn't grab the hosel and pull the ball left and into possibly deeper trouble.

SHOT RECIPE	
CLUB	Wedge or 9-iron
AIM	Right of target
STANCE	Stand closer to ball
BALL POSITION	Between center & right foot
SWING	Full backswing, limited finish
FEEL	Pull handle down from top

DIFFICULTY LEVEL

0	1	2	3	4	5

Catch this one anything but perfectly solid and you'll be hitting your next shot from the junk as well.

TIGHTEN UP
- Thick rough will yank the clubface left through impact.
- If your normal grip pressure is a "7," make your grip here a solid "10."

82

CHECK!
When you play the ball back in your stance, it's easy to lean away from the target. Make sure your shoulders are level.

CLUB OPTIONS

- If you can see the top half of your ball, use your 9-iron (stronger players can use an 8-iron).
- If only a small circle on the top of the ball is visible, opt for your sand wedge.

GET CLOSER

- Stand closer to the ball. This makes your club more upright, helping you to hit down on the ball and minimize turf contact.

HIT AND QUIT

- The rough likely will stop your swing just after impact.
- Focus on what's happening before you strike the ball, not after.

HOW TO GOUGE IT FROM THE JUNK

Grip the club tightly.

Step 1

Stand closer to the ball and choke down a few inches on the handle. Notice how this makes your shaft more upright (a good thing in this situation). Aim slightly right of where you want the ball to land.

Start your swing by hinging your wrists.

Step 3

Hinge the club back quickly. On normal swings you start hinging your wrists when your hands reach hip height. Here, you want fully cocked wrists by the time your hands reach thigh height.

Play the ball back.

Step 2

Play the ball back and increase your grip pressure. If you don't have a firm hold on the club the grass will turn it over and the ball will go left. Forward-press your hands so the shaft leans toward the target.

KEY MOVE

Pull the handle of the club down to the ball.

Step 4

From the top, swing down sharply and with plenty of force. Feel like you're pulling the handle of the club down into the ball. Keep your legs quiet (notice how little they move in Steps 3 and 4).

The Rules Guy

Shotmaking by the Book

Yeah, it moved, but I swear I didn't touch it!

I'm sure you didn't, but you might have touched a long blade of grass that also was in contact with the ball, and that's what caused it to move. This happens a lot in the rough, and since the ball is down and only you can see it, it's your move to call the infraction on yourself if it occurs. **When the ball moves after you take your address— even if your club never touched the ball— you need to place the ball in its original spot and swallow a one-stroke penalty.** We know, it's not fair, but as John F. Kennedy once said, "Life's not fair." (He's believed to have made this remark on his way to visiting a Hollywood starlet after carding a 74.) If the ball moves after you begin your stroke, that's a penalty situation, too. In this instance, however, you don't have to replace the ball. You can play the shot but add to it a one-stroke penalty.

This rule (No. 18) applies everywhere on the course, from the tee box to the green and all points in between. In order to completely avoid the threat of a penalty, hover your club above the grass—don't sole it—and start your swing from there. Treat it like a bunker situation, where it's illegal to ground your club. You don't want to take any chances, especially since you're not in an ideal place to make up for any lost strokes or penalties.

83

SHOT

43 The Hardpan Smash

An easy swing can get you home from bare, hard ground

84

What It Is
A power play from the dirt.

When to Use it
When you've missed the fairway and rough altogether and landed in hardpan (a catch-all term to describe densely packed dirt), but close enough to the green to think about going for it.

How to Hit It
If there's one good thing about hardpan it's that your ball can't sink into it. The ball will always sit up, and if its position allows you to take your stance and make a swing without bumping into any obstacles, then this is a pretty straightforward play.

DIFFICULTY LEVEL

| 0 | 1 | 2 | 3 | 4 | 5 |

Make contact at the right point and the only setback is a gouge mark on the sole of your club.

SMOOTH MOVE
- Since you won't be able to dig your spikes in the ground and get some traction, keep your swing smooth.
- Take your hands back only to shoulder height, stay centered over the ball and don't try to kill it.

CONTACT POINT
- The secret to this shot is to make contact with the ball and the hardpan at the same time.
- If you hit the ground first, your club will bounce hard off the dirt and catch only the top half of the ball.

CHECK!
Shuffle your feet on top of the hardpan like you do in sand. Your feet won't dig, but you'll need all the stability you can get.

AVOID A DIG

- Notice how the shoulders, hips and knees are facing the target. Turning like this guarantees you won't come down too steep and stick the club in the ground.

SHOT RECIPE	
CLUB	A hybrid or high-lofted FW
AIM	At target
STANCE	Weight slightly on left side
BALL POSITION	Center
SWING	¾ back to full finish
FEEL	Hit ball and dirt at same time

HOW TO HAMMER IT FROM HARDPAN

Use one of your hybrids.

Aim here.

Ball in the center, weight slightly left.

Step 1

If the distance allows, use one of your hybrids (choke down if you're inside your hybrid range). The extra loft on these clubs makes this shot easier. Position the ball in the middle of your stance.

Step 2

Set your weight so that it *slightly* favors your left side. If your weight is too far forward, you'll have the tendency to swing too steeply, causing the club to stick in the dirt.

Swing short and easy— the ground is too slick to go hard after it.

KEY MOVE

Hit the ball and the dirt at the same time.

Step 3

You have plenty of club in your hands, so make a comfortable, three-quarter backswing. As you swing back, try to remain centered over the ball.

Step 4

Just like how you aim for a spot two inches behind the ball when hitting shots from sand, aim for the dirt just behind the ball. Your goal is to strike the ball and the hardpan at the same time.

85

SHOT

44

How to Hit Off a Cart Path

Give the ball a ride from the most unusual lie

86

The Situation
The ball has come to rest on a cart path. Normally, you'd take your free drop, but if you drop it here you'll be playing from the bushes. You'd rather hit it off cement—and you should.

The Solution
As you study each of the shots in this book you'll discover that several of them call for "ball-first" contact *[for example Shot 45 on the opposite page]*. You're thinking, "duh." Yes, your club should strike the ball before it contacts the turf on most shots (it doesn't in sand), but in the ball-first scenarios, it's *critical* that it happen in that order. If not, you've got a disaster on your hands, and the cart-path lie is no exception.

How to Hit It
Make a few practice swings in nearby grass with the goal of just nipping the tops of the blades. Once you get a feel for the swing, address the ball on the path and copy the moves at right.

DIFFICULTY LEVEL

0	1	2	3	4	5

Your timing and contact need to be perfect, but since this technically is a save situation, even bad impact will get you back into play.

AIM LEFT
- The taller you stand, the more likely the ball will fade, so aim a few yards left of your target.
- Just because it's on cart path doesn't mean you should baby the shot. Use the biggest swing that allows you to keep your balance.

STAND TALL
- The last thing you want is to catch this shot fat, so stand taller (bend less from your hips).
- Choke down on the club for this same reason.

WEIGHT SHIFT
- Notice how the right foot is raising up on its toe and the left foot is planted.
- That tells you that weight is shifting forward so you don't catch the path behind the ball.

SHOT RECIPE	
CLUB	Any iron
AIM	Slightly left
STANCE	Slightly open
BALL POSITION	Center
SWING	Favor balance over speed
FEEL	Practice "nipping" the grass

45

Power It From Pine Straw

The real trouble is moving the ball before you swing

The Situation

You've strayed from the fairway and ended up in some pine straw under a grove of trees. The ball is up and you're able to take a normal stance and make a full swing, but you're not sure if you should hit down to get the ball out or sweep it off the straw.

The Solution

First, take care addressing the ball. Pine straw can be quite slippery, not only in terms of footing but from a rules standpoint as well. If you nudge any straw touching your ball and cause it to move, you incur a one-stroke penalty. Play it safe and don't sole the club. Hover it an inch off the ground at address *[inset photo, right]*, standing a bit taller than normal to compensate. Then, copy the moves at right.

SHOT RECIPE	
CLUB	Variable
AIM	At target
STANCE	Standard
BALL POSITION	Standard
SWING	Try to sweep it
FEEL	Your feet are in cement

DIFFICULTY LEVEL

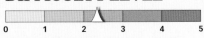

| 0 | 1 | 2 | 3 | 4 | 5 |

The lie looks trickier than it is. You'll get full power as long as you keep your footing.

GO FOR IT
- You can hit anything from a sand wedge to a hybrid from this lie. You may be off the fairway, but you can still get the ball on the green.

PLANT IT
- To shore up your footing, pretend you're wearing a pair of cement shoes. Plant your feet and keep your weight centered as you swing.
- If you keep your lower body quiet, you can remain steady and make solid contact.

SWEEP IT
- Regardless of the club you've chosen, the most important thing to remember is that you make ball-first contact. It's the same principle as playing a shot of a cart path, oddly enough. Sweep the ball off the straw instead of hitting down on it.

87

SHOT

46 How to Catch It Clean From Wet Ground

Treat this shot like you would a blast from a fairway bunker

The Situation
The weather's fine but previous rain has left the course a bit soft—you're splashing up water on every swing and having a hard time making crisp contact.

The Solution
Hitting from wet ground is not too different from hitting from a fairway bunker. In both situations you're standing on soft ground and you need to make ball-first contact or the ball will go nowhere. *Follow the steps at right.*

88

TALL BOY
- Address the ball with a more upright posture to offset the fact your feet have sunk into the soft ground.

AIM HERE
- Pick a spot on the ground just in front of the ball and try to hit it. This will help you produce ball-first contact and avoid the soggy turf.

TIMED IMPACT
- Try to get your right knee and the clubhead to the ball at the same time.
- This gives you the cleanest possible contact.

DIFFICULTY LEVEL

0   1   2   3   4   5

If you can hit solid fairway bunker shots, then this one is a piece of cake.

HOW TO PINCH THE BALL OFF SOGGY TURF

Step 1

Take a bunker setup
When you address the ball from this lie, your feet will sink down into the soft turf, just like they do when you swing from the sand. To offset the fact that your swing arc has been lowered, grip down on the handle a solid inch. Position the ball in the center of your stance (or just forward of center if you're hitting a long iron or hybrid).

Step 2

Hover your clubhead
Stand taller to the ball (don't bend as much from your hips) so that you can comfortably hover the club above the ground and line up the leading edge with the ball's equator.

Step 3

Hit the grass in front of the ball
Before you start your swing, aim for a spot on the grass one inch in front of the ball. Your goal is to hit the back of the ball then drive your club into that spot. This gives you ball-first contact and negates any interference from the wet ground under your feet. As you swing into impact, **picture your clubhead and right knee reaching the ball at the same time**. (If your knee gets there first, you'll catch it fat; if your club gets there first, you'll hit it thin.)

89

Pick a spot one inch ahead of the ball, then drive your clubhead through the back of the ball and into that spot.

CHECK!
You can take relief from casual water (outside a hazard), but the water must be visible before or after you take your stance.

SHOT RECIPE	
CLUB	Variable
AIM	At target
STANCE	Standard
BALL POSITION	Center
SWING	Full back to full finish
FEEL	Aim for grass in front of ball

SHOT 47

Feet In Bunker, Ball On Grass

Treat it as a regular shot but from a slippery stance

The Situation
Your feet are in the sand and the ball is resting on a grassy slope.

The Solution
Use your trusty pitch swing but with a slightly different address position because the ball is slightly above your feet and you're not on solid ground.
Follow the steps at right:

SHOT RECIPE	
CLUB	Sand wedge
AIM	Left of target
STANCE	Open
BALL POSITION	Slightly back of center
SWING	Wristy backswing
FEEL	Point clubface at sky

DIFFICULTY LEVEL

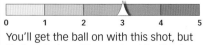

0   1   2   3   4   5

You'll get the ball on with this shot, but likely not close. Your main objective is to not dump the ball in the bunker.

VERY RISKY   RISKY   SAFE

PLAN A SMART PATH
- Before you address the ball, take a few seconds to **think about your best route to safety.** Because of your unusual stance, your goal should be to simply get this shot on the green. So be careful. If the pin isn't tucked into a corner of the green and you have enough landing room, you can go right at it. But if you have doubts, don't be afraid to aim away from the flag and toward the fattest part of the green.
- Above all, you want to make sure your next shot is a putt, so don't take foolish chances.

HOW TO HIT A PITCH WITH YOUR FEET IN THE SAND

Step 1

Match your setup to the slope
You need to get comfortable at address in order to make solid contact. Follow these setup keys:
1 **Grip down on the club** by a couple of inches because the ball is above your feet.
2 **Open the clubface** slightly at address to get more loft and combat the slope, which will tend to pull the ball left.
3 **Play the ball** just behind the center of your stance to encourage a steeper downswing path.
4 **Dig your feet down** about 1 inch into the sand for stability, and anchor about 60 percent of your weight over your left foot.

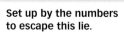

Set up by the numbers to escape this lie.

Step 2

Take a last look

You've made the changes to your setup to fit the nature of the shot, so now it's time to take a final look at your landing spot. **Keep your knees flexed and waggle the club above the grass,** which will help you minimize tension in your arms and lower body. Focus on the landing spot you've selected, and picture the flight of the ball as it flies toward that spot.

Step 3

Hinge back

On the backswing, hinge the club back a little more than you would on a normal pitch. **You want to get some elevation right at the start,** because it's easy from this type of lie to swing more around your body and get the club way behind you. In this situation, you need a steeper angle of attack so that the club catches as little grass as possible before making contact with the ball. This will help keep the momentum of your swing going forward so the ball gets up in the air.

Step 4

Swing to the target

Resist the temptation to swing right of your target in an effort to get more height on the shot. That's why you opened the clubface at address—to counter the effect of the hill and get the ball airborne. So go ahead and swing through to the target, and try to **hold the clubface up toward the sky** as you pass impact.

DANGER!
This is not a "hack-it-out" situation. Make a balanced, rhythmic swing and the ball will end up safely on the green.

91

48

Restricted Forward-Swing

Recoil at impact to bust the ball (not your club)

What It Is
A regular punch swing that doesn't have a follow-through.

When to Use It
For those curse-causing situations when the ball comes to rest at the base of a tree or other obstacle from which you cannot take relief without taking a penalty. You can make a full backswing, but you can't follow through without slamming the club into the trunk or the impediment.

How to Hit It
Most golfers try to swing slow here, but that leads to mis-hits (usually in the form of fat contact with the ball dribbling only a few yards forward). Keep your speed the same, but make a smaller swing so you can pull the club back at impact.

BURY IT
- If you're not comfortable with pulling the club back after impact (or your wrists won't allow it), then simply bury the club in the dirt at impact and leave it there, like you do when trying to blast from a buried bunker lie.

DIFFICULTY LEVEL

0 1 2 3 4 5

You're just looking to make contact without damaging you or your club. The only difficult parts are a funky stance and ball position.

92

WRIST AT TARGET

- Since you're only making a little half swing with zero follow-through, make sure the back of your left hand points where you want the ball to go as you strike it. Unless your grip is unusually weak or strong, your clubface will point in the same direction as the back of your left hand.

STEEP CONTACT

- Come down sharply on the ball, like you're trying to pound it into the ground.
- Make sure that all of your weight is over your left foot at impact or you'll catch the shot fat.

SHOT RECIPE	
CLUB	Short to mid-iron
AIM	Standard
STANCE	Shoulder-width
BALL POSITION	Close to center as possible
SWING	Half back, stop at impact
FEEL	Pull back the club at impact

HOW TO PUNCH A RESTRICTED SWING

Step 1

Select one of your mid- or short irons (a shorter club is easier to control because it doesn't travel as fast), take a shoulder-width stance and play the ball as close to the middle as possible.

Step 2

Take your club back by hinging your wrists quickly and fully so that the clubhead gets above your hands almost immediately. Swing your hands back only to hip height (your goal is to advance the ball from this lie, not hole it out).

Step 3

Swing your arms sharply down on the ball, as if you're trying to take a deep divot. Keep your speed up or you'll risk hitting the shot fat. As soon as you make contact, pull the club away from the target. Make the club recoil like it just hit a tire. That'll stop you from striking the trunk while still getting plenty of juice on the ball.

DANGER!
Clubs can—and will—break after striking large objects. If you have any doubts, take a drop or play a short chip shot.

You may be forced to play the ball off your front foot. That's okay. Just set more weight forward.

Set the clubhead higher than your hands in your half-backswing.

KEY MOVE

Pull back at impact as if your club has struck a tire.

93

SHOT 49

Restricted Backswing

Here's how to advance it when you can't take the club all the way back

The Situation
Your ball is up against a tree or other obstacle that prevents you from making a complete backswing.

The Solution
Don't go from worse to worst. Look at what you can reasonably accomplish and avoid a double penalty. In most situations like this your only play is a less-than-full punch swing. Follow the steps at right to catch the ball as cleanly as possible and get it back in play.

SHOT RECIPE	
CLUB	Short iron
AIM	At target
STANCE	Narrow
BALL POSITION	Slightly left of center
SWING	At 60% speed
FEEL	Brush the ground

DIFFICULTY LEVEL

0	1	2	3	4	5

Since you're using a high-lofted club, all you need to do is make good contact and the ball will go up.

GET PREPPED
- Make at least 10 practice strokes.
- With each rehearsal, feel how far you can take the club back and concentrate on making as smooth a transition as possible.

GET GROUNDED
- The mistake here is rushing your transition (easy to do since you're cutting your backswing way short). As soon as you do this, your chances of catching the shot thin skyrocket.
- Your goal is to brush the ground underneath the ball. Do that and the shot will take care of itself.

94

HOW TO ESCAPE WITH ONLY HALF A SWING

Step 1

Plan a safe route
Look around and see what's possible. Likely, there won't be much. In most instances your goal should be to get the ball back in the fairway.

Step 2

Get set
Make sure you select the correct club with enough loft to get you over any obstacles or rough. The longest club you should use is a 7-iron. Set up square to where you want the ball to land with a narrower stance than normal.

Step 3

Rehearse a half-swing
Choke down and make several practice swings. A Tour player will make 10 to 15 practice strokes when hitting an unfamiliar shot like this. Make enough practice strokes so that you know that you won't hit the tree [photos, right] and you can brush the ground.

Step 4

Build some trust
At the end of your practice strokes, get comfortable in your setup, flex your knees and commit to the shot. Focus on making solid contact and a full follow-through. You've hit punch shots thousands of times—this one is no different.

KEY MOVE

Make several practice swings to find out how far back you can take your club.

This is an all-arms shot that needs a soft transition from backswing to downswing.

Trapped Under a Tree? Use Your Putter!

Pop down on the ball and watch it run

You may not think much about your putter until you reach the green, but the flatstick can be a tremendously versatile trouble club elsewhere on the course.

The next time you find yourself in a spot where it's hard to get a regular iron on the ball out to the fairway or onto the green, try this. Position the ball roughly 12 inches to the right of your right foot. Swing your putter back with a lot of wrist action and then pop the putterhead down hard on the back of the ball. The ball will shoot out low with a lot of topspin, which will allow it to cover a lot of distance without much effort.

Practice this shot to get a feel for how much force is needed for a variety of distances, and then head out to the course armed with a very handy new weapon.

Bring the putter down hard on the back of the ball.

95

SHOT

50 Punch Shot Through Trees

If you have a gap, this low-flying laser
will get you back in the open

96

GAP CHECK

- Don't try to hit through too narrow an opening.
- If you don't have at least three yards between two trees, look for another opening, especially if there's some distance between you and the gap.

BALL BACK

- Since you're in the trees, your lie might be a little cushy. Play the ball farther back in your stance to make sure you strike it before anything else.
- Playing the ball back also ensures that you hit it on a lower trajectory.

LEFT HAND LOW

- You'll want this shot to release and run out toward the green, so make an aggressive release.
- Get the back of your left hand pointing at the ground after impact.

DIFFICULTY LEVEL

0   1   2   3   4   5

It's really important to keep the clubhead behind your hands at impact. If you typically scoop at the ball, you might not keep the ball low enough.

SHOT RECIPE	
CLUB	Mid- to long iron
AIM	Through ample gap
STANCE	Standard
BALL POSITION	Back of center
SWING	Half back to half finish
FEEL	Flat swing and strong release

What It Is

A controlled, low-flying shot that only gets a few yards off the ground and runs like crazy when it hits the turf.

When to Use It

From the trees, but only if there's a gap on a line toward the green with enough wiggle room for you to play through without much risk. The farther from you the gap is, the wider it must be since every yard the ball moves the greater the chance it has to go off line.

How to Hit It

Think about what you need in this situation:

1. A shot that flies very low
Obviously, you don't want to catch any low-hanging branches. You want a screamer that hugs the ground [see Step 1].

2. A shot that comes off with very little backspin
A spinning ball rises—a big no-no in this situation. Think knuckle ball, not curve [see Step 2].

3. Lots of roll
You're not going to get your full distance with this swing, so the ball must come out extra-hot, getting you as close to the green as possible [see Step 3].

F.Y.I.
This technique works great for any situation where you need to keep the ball low. It can also help fix your slice.

HOW TO HIT IT THROUGH A GAP

Stay away from your short irons and wedges. Loft is a killer in this situation.

Trace a flatter swing path (below your shoulders).

Point the club left of target in your follow-through.

Step 1

To keep the ball low...
...adjust your setup. Select a club you're confident will stay beneath the overhang (probably nothing higher than a 6-iron). Take your normal stance and posture with the ball positioned just back of center.

Step 2

To reduce spin...
...make a short, flat backswing. Try to swing the club more behind you and keep the shaft below your right shoulder.

Step 3

To make it run once it hits...
...juice up your release. Turn your hands over strongly through impact. The back of your left wrist should face the ground after impact with the club pointing left of your target.

97

SHOT 51

Approach Over an Obstacle

Who put that tree there? Who cares! Here's how to go right over it.

98

The Situation
You're only 150 yards or so from the green but there's a tree on your most direct line to the flagstick.

The Solution
The standard, by-the-book advice when you're behind a tree is to play safely out to the fairway. But what if you're down in your match and need to make something happen? Or it's the 18th hole and you need a par to break 90 for the first time. With a few tweaks, you should be able to throw your ball up high over that tall boy and keep your momentum going.

DIFFICULTY LEVEL

0	1	2	3	4	5

If the lie is good and you nail your setup, this shot should present zero challenge, even to high-handicappers.

GO FOR IT!
- Take dead aim at the tree or the obstacle in your way and set up to the ball as if you were hitting a big, high fade.
- This is something that should feel familiar to many of you, and will help the ball gain height quickly.

If you have any doubt, take one less club to make sure you'll clear the obstacle.

HOW TO FLY OVER OBSTACLES

Step 1

Assess your lie
The most important question to ask yourself is, "Do I have enough space to clear this tree?" It's impossible to determine without first looking at your lie. You'll be in the rough, so hopefully it's not too thick. You need a somewhat clean lie to pull off this shot.
- If half of the ball is sitting on top of the grass, go for it.
- If only a quarter of the ball is visible, use no more than a pitching wedge.
- If the ball is sitting down low, don't even try it.

Step 2

Set up to create loft
Let's say you have 150 yards to the green, normally a 7-iron, but you need the loft of an 8-iron to clear the tree. Take the 7-iron and make these adjustments.
- Widen your stance so the insides of your feet are just outside your shoulders.
- Aim the clubface at the target, then align your feet about 10 degrees open.
- Play the ball an inch more forward than normal.

Take an extra-wide stance.

Step 3

Make a steep backswing

Feel like the clubhead is outside your hands as it nears hip height in your backswing *[see right]*. This will be easier to accomplish after the adjustments you made to your setup. Even if the clubhead isn't actually outside your hands, trying to get it there will open the clubface. Your swing will feel steeper than normal, like you're lifting the club straight up as you reach the top. The goal is to produce a downswing with enough force to help the ball jump up and fly in a hurry.

Step 4

Keep the face open

Try to keep the clubface open for as long as possible. To do this, think about folding your arms quickly to get the club pointing at the sky *[see photo, above right]*. This is a vertical release, and if you slice the ball it should feel very natural. (In fact, slicers have a distinct advantage hitting over a tree, due to their steep swings). Make a few practice swings to get the hang of this vertical release. At impact, it should feel as if the club is in contact with the grass for only a moment before coming back up.

CHECK!
If your ball is in a fluffy lie in the rough, there's no need to club down since the longer grass causes the shot to come out "hot."

KEY MOVE
Fold your arms up quickly after impact rather than extending them out.

Keep the clubhead outside your hands on your takeaway.

DON'T DO THIS
• On a normal shot you release the club so the toe passes the heel and your arms extend the club low past impact. This is exactly what you don't want when hitting over a tree.

99

SHOT RECIPE	
CLUB	One extra club
AIM	At target
STANCE	Open (fade stance)
BALL POSITION	Slightly forward of standard
SWING	Full backswing to full finish
FEEL	Fold arms after impact

SHOT

52 Punch-Out From Your Knees

It's not a comedy skit, it's a par-saver!

What It Is
A recovery shot you hit while kneeling on the ground.

When to Use It
When you can't reach the ball with your normal stance because the ball lies under an obstruction (in this example, an angled tree trunk).

How to Hit It
Grab your shortest hybrid or fairway wood, drop to your knees and follow the steps at right.

HANDS LEAD

- Make sure your hands get to the ball before your clubhead. Otherwise this shot will hook wildly to the left.

WOODS ONLY

- A short iron might be easier to control, but with its long hosel set so close to the ground, you'll dig it into the turf way before the ball.

SHOT RECIPE	
CLUB	Shortest hybrid or wood
AIM	At target
STANCE	From your knees
BALL POSITION	Center
SWING	Baseball-type
FEEL	Lead the club with your hands

DIFFICULTY LEVEL

0 1 2 3 4 5

You've likely never practiced this shot, so the feeling will be strange.

100

HEY, BATTER!
• Make a level swing, like you're swinging a baseball bat.

HOW TO BUST ONE FROM YOUR KNEES

Drop down to your knees and **spread them as far as you can to establish a solid base** (flare both feet out if you can to make your stance even more stable). Grab your shortest fairway wood or hybrid and choke down all the way to the base of the handle. (Don't use an iron—the ultra-flat shaft arrangement makes it easy for the long hosel on an iron to dig into the ground at impact).

As you settle into position, notice how far the clubface points to the left when you sole your club behind the ball (it happens automatically when you make the shaft flatter). It'll look strange, but don't change it. **If you keep your hands ahead of the clubhead through impact, the face will square up and the ball will fly straight**.

The big mistake here is allowing the clubhead to drop down, causing you to hit the ground behind the ball. It's difficult to think about swing plane with such an extreme setup, so hover the club above the ball at address. This allows you to make clean contact even if the clubhead drops down.

Try to make a baseball swing back and through. Obviously, this is an arms-only motion. Make sure to hinge your wrists and swing your left arm across your chest on your backswing, and release the club across your left shoulder. You'll be surprised how much distance you'll generate.

Hover the club at address.

Swing your left arm across your chest.

Swing all the way through.

Add some wrist hinge.

Point the shaft left of target.

Keep your hands ahead of the club at impact.

Finish over your left shoulder.

The Rules Guy

Shotmaking by the Book

"Hit *that* shot? I don't think so."

So your tee shot ends up against a tree or behind a rock or in a vast underground chasm—any place where you can't hit the damn thing. Your options are to grab that left-handed sand wedge you carry just for situations like this, or deem your ball unplayable. If you declare your ball unplayable, you can exercise one of three options:

A) **Play a ball as near as possible to the spot from which the original ball was last played;**

B) **Drop a ball behind the point where the ball lies, keeping that point directly between the hole and the spot on which the ball is dropped, with no limit on how far behind that point the ball may be dropped; or**

C) **Drop a ball within two club-lengths of the spot where the ball lies, but not nearer the hole.**

The best advice we can give is that if you think your ball might be unplayable, it is. You're not Phil Mickelson, or even Phil Blackmar—the odds of pulling off a miracle shot from the junk are slim. So take your one-stroke medicine and try to make a putt and save par. The rules for declaring an unplayable lie in a bunker are the same, but in option B and C you must drop in the bunker, which proves the old adage, "A high-handicap and sand are not soon parted."

101

Bunker

Escaping the Sand

The pros make sand shots look easy. Here's how to do likewise, even from lies where you usually leave the ball in the bunker.

EVEN IF YOU FOLLOW the standard advice for escaping a bunker (hit behind the ball and let it fly out on a cushion of sand), you're not guaranteed a successful escape. That's because it's good only for a standard bunker lie, which is difficult to define considering the many types of sand, the many ways the ball can bury itself in the sand, and the inherent shape of a sand bunker. Pick a spot in any bunker and within a 2-foot radius you'll find an uphill lie, a downhill lie, as well as lies with the ball below and above your feet. In this chapter you'll learn what it takes to get the ball out and onto the green from every conceivable situation, including the ones that appear inescapable. So dig in and swing—just don't ground your club.

SHOT

53

Standard Greenside Bunker Shot

Take a big swing and a lot of sand for a fail-safe escape

The Situation

You've landed smack in the middle of a greenside bunker with the ball sitting up on the sand. You've been here many times before but haven't had the consistent success on bunker shots that builds confidence.

The Solution

Your key thought on this shot should be to "splash" the ball out. You want the club to enter the sand first and skim underneath the ball. The biggest protection against missing is to make an aggressive swing and displace a lot of sand.

SHOT RECIPE	
CLUB	Sand wedge
AIM	Slightly left of target
STANCE	Slightly open
BALL POSITION	Between center and left heel
SWING	Full back to full finish
FEEL	"Splash" the ball out

DIFFICULTY LEVEL

| 0 | 1 | 2 | 3 | 4 | 5 |

The standard bunker blast should be a cinch. It's one of the few shots where you actually need to miss the ball.

DISTANCE CHECK
- Before teeing off, hit a few balls from the practice bunker using your sand wedge. See how far they travel with your regular full swing.
- This gives you a baseline for all distances you'll face during play.

DIVOT ADJUST
- To reach a pin beyond your full-swing sand-wedge distance, take a shallower divot (like you're skimming the surface).
- To land close to a pin placed short of your full-swing sand-wedge distance, shorten your backswing and take more sand.

HOW TO ESCAPE THE BUNKER EVERY TIME

Step 1

• Use your sand wedge and set up to the ball with the clubface square (or slightly open) and with a slightly open stance (toe line pointing about 10 feet left of your target).
• Dig your feet into the sand and get a feel for its texture. Is it soft, hard, heavy, etc.? *[See Shot 57 for what the answer means].*

Step 2

Aim a few feet left of the hole, but don't overdo it. Most players cut across the ball too much on bunker shots; this shot should actually feel like your normal swing.

Step 2

Make a three-quarter backswing with a full body rotation. On your downswing, try to enter the sand two or three inches behind the ball and leave a dollar-bill-sized divot (or even bigger) in the sand. Focus on making an aggressive swing and a full follow-through to splash the ball out.

CHECK!
Hitting 2" behind the ball is good rule to follow. If you're taking too much sand, focus on exiting the sand 2" in front of the ball.

Note ball position: **slightly forward of where your swing bottoms out.**

KEY MOVE

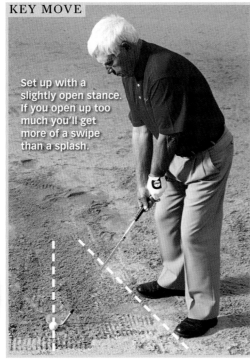

Set up with a slightly open stance. If you open up too much you'll get more of a swipe than a splash.

How to Practice a Perfect Bunker Swing

You don't need any sand to do it!

Think of your ball in the bunker as a three-layer cake: The ball is the first layer, the sand is the second layer and the base of the bunker is the third. The trick is to cut the second layer out without touching the first or third.

Try this drill. Place a ball on a tee, as high as if you were going to hit your driver *[photo, below right]*. Take your address position with your sand wedge and open the clubface. Now make your regular bunker swing and try to hit the tee away so the ball just drops at your feet *[photo, below left]*.

Why It Works: This drill forces you to keep the club level to the ground on both sides of the ball. If you hit the ball, you're probably attempting to hit up too much. Once you get good at this, try teeing the ball lower. This will help you make contact with the sand closer to the ball, which allows you to nip it and put extra spin on it.

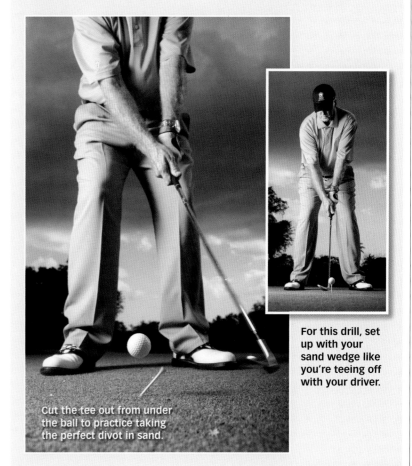

Cut the tee out from under the ball to practice taking the perfect divot in sand.

For this drill, set up with your sand wedge like you're teeing off with your driver.

105

54

How To Unplug a Plugged Lie

Burying your club is bad news on normal sand shots, but it's a winner when the ball is plugged

106

The Situation

Your ball is three-quarters buried in loose sand toward the upper part of a steep lip. Even taking a stance won't be easy. You'll have no trouble swinging the club back, but deep sand and the overhanging lip will severely limit your follow-through.

The Solution

Realistically, you can't do much more to the ball than dislodge it. But guess what? That's about all you have to do! In fact, you're free to commit the most common bunker error of all time and quit on the shot. More good news? You get to make a violent, hard, no-finish swing and pound that stupid bunker!

DIFFICULTY LEVEL

| 0 | 1 | 2 | 3 | 4 | 5 |

Not many swings get easier than just slamming your clubhead into the sand. The only trouble is distance control.

F.Y.I.
You *accelerate* on this shot. That's different from when you quit on it unintentionally and leave the ball in the sand.

If the ball is only half-buried, use the same technique, but close the face and don't slam the club into the sand as hard. But when it's buried like this, pound that stupid bunker!

DROP ANCHOR
- Stabilize your back foot by digging it much deeper into the sand than your front foot.

ZERO RELEASE
- Don't try to turn your right arm over your left after impact because any follow-through will be minimal.

SHIFT FORWARD
- Be sure to keep most of your weight on your left side.

DIG A HOLE
- Your clubhead should literally burrow into the sand directly beneath the ball.

SHOT RECIPE	
CLUB	Sand wedge
AIM	At target
STANCE	Square, weight forward
BALL POSITION	Between center and left foot
SWING	Full to impact then stop
FEEL	Bury the club in the sand

HOW TO POUND IT OUT

Step 1

Use whichever of your wedges has the most bounce and open the blade just a bit at address. As you finish settling into your posture, dig your back foot deeper in the sand than your front.

Dig in...

Step 2

Make a full backswing, then slam the club powerfully into the sand an inch or two behind your ball as if you're trying to bury the clubhead.

KEY MOVE

...bury the clubhead...

Step 3

Don't expect any follow-through, just a soft rebound effect as your club emerges lazily from the bunker. Meanwhile your ball and a half-cup of sand are already crossing the bunker lip on their way to the green.

...and leave it there.

107

SHOT 55

How to Beat a Fried-Egg Lie

Swing hard to blast it out soft

108

The Situation

Your approach shot landed in a greenside bunker, and the ball came to rest in the depression it made in the sand. Your normal bunker swing won't work here since the mini-crater your ball sits in prevents you from floating the ball out on the proverbial "cushion of sand."

The Solution

Take a steeper angle of approach and don't follow through. Instead, make a big explosion and leave your club in the sand.

That's depressing.

DIFFICULTY LEVEL

0	1	2	3	4	5

It's like hitting a ball out of a divot and out of the sand at the same time. If you don't dig down, you're in for very thin contact.

KEY MOVE

BURY CLUB
- Instead of making your normal follow-through, bury your club in the bunker and create an explosion of sand, just like you do when the ball is plugged [Shot 54].
- The ball will come out hot and run farther than a regular bunker shot, but you'll be on the green.

HINGE SWING
- Take a steeper-than-normal backswing with a lot of wrist hinge (you want shorter arm action for this shot).
- Hit down into the sand an inch or so behind the ball.

WEIGHT LEFT
- Address the ball as you would for a regular greenside bunker shot.
- Open your stance, but move more weight onto your front leg and square up the clubface so it can dig straight into the sand.

SHOT RECIPE	
CLUB	Sand wedge
AIM	Slightly left of target
STANCE	Slightly open
BALL POSITION	Between center and left foot
SWING	Full with lots of hinge
FEEL	You're coming in too steep

SHOT 56
Semi-Buried Lie

Hinge your wrists and then hold them to dig your ball out

The Situation
Your ball is half-buried in a greenside bunker. From this lie, the ball will fly relatively low and run out when it hits the green. A high bunker lip will make this shot even tougher.

The Solution
The key to hitting this shot is to create a downward angle of attack. You need to hinge your wrists in your backswing and keep them firm at impact to dig the club into the sand.

DIFFICULTY LEVEL

0 1 2 3 4 5

You can't know how the ball will react on the green with all the variables. When playing to a tight pin, you should be happy just landing this on the green.

The semi-buried lie.

KEY MOVE

HINGE / HOLD
- To blast the ball out when it's only slightly buried, use the "hinge-and-hold" swing.
- Hinge your wrists fully going back, and keep them hinged on your downswing.

Pinch in your knees and set your clubface square to your target.

ENTER HERE
- Unlike regular sand shots where you hit 1 to 2 inches behind the ball, enter the sand just at the back of the ball
- Feel like you're striking both sand and the ball at the same time.

HOW TO DO IT

Step 1
Grab your sand wedge and set up with the ball back toward your right foot and the shaft angled forward.

Step 2
Take a narrow stance, which gets your weight on your left side, and pinch in your knees. Check that your sternum is in front of the ball, and your clubface is square to help you dig into the sand.

Step 3
Make a hinge-and-hold swing, hinging your wrists on the backswing and holding them firm on contact. You don't want to have any play at all with your wrists and hands to preserve that downward angle of attack you've achieved.

Step 4
Make a fairly aggressive swing and try to enter the sand as close to the ball as you can, as if you're hitting them both at the same time. And don't make your normal follow-through. You should feel like you're leaving the club in the sand and all the energy of your swing has gone toward digging the ball out.

109

SHOT RECIPE	
CLUB	Sand wedge
AIM	At target
STANCE	Narrow, weight on left foot
BALL POSITION	Back of center
SWING	3/4 back to 3/4 finish
FEEL	Firm hands

SHOTS

57 & 58 Blast From the Fluff or Tough

How to gauge the sand beneath your feet and make the right impression

110

FLUFFY SAND

- Your club will tend to stick in the bunker because of the weight of the material it must dislodge.
- Hitting a good explosion from here means taking a very large divot with a very fast swing.

NORMAL SAND

- The ball will carry farther than a shot hit from fluffy sand and shorter than a shot hit from thin sand (as long as swing speed remains the same).

THIN SAND

- There's less material your club can extract so the ball will come out "hot."
- From this lie, you need the least energy to get the ball to the hole.

DIFFICULTY LEVEL

0   1   2   3   4   5

If your everyday bunker swing is sound, then changing speeds to match the depth of sand you're in is easy.

The Situation

You're so desperate to get out of the bunker that you never give much thought to the type of sand you're playing from. This creates trouble because no two bunkers are alike. Some are filled with so much sand that you almost sink when you step into them. Others are so thin you feel like you're standing on cement. When you use the swing that gets you out of fluffy bunkers on a thin lie, the ball will go screaming across the green.

The Solution

The secret to hitting successful bunker shots regardless of where you play (or how little the superintendent takes care of the course) is to adjust your speed to match the depth of sand. Check the sand types at left to find out if you need to swing harder (fluffy sand) or slower (thin sand).

DANGER!
When judging the depth of sand, don't swipe the sand with your club or feet. That's "testing a hazard"—a two-stroke penalty.

HOW TO SWING FASTER (OR SOFTER) IN A BUNKER

The simplest way to add speed—or take some off—is to make different-sized swings both back and through. Don't try to memorize or measure these specific swing lengths—all you need is an overall feel for small, medium and large

FLUFFY

FROM A FLUFFY LIE...
...swing three-quarters back to a full finish. This will give you 10 yards in the air with 2 yards of roll with your sand wedge.

THIN

FROM A THIN LIE...
...swing from hip-high back to hip-high through. This will give you 10 yards in the air with 2 yards of roll with your sand wedge.

111

NORMAL

FROM A NORMAL LIE...
...swing half-back to half-through (chest-to-chest). This will give you 10 yards in the air with 2 yards of roll with your sand wedge.

KEEP IT CONSISTENT

When changing speeds, keep your setup exactly the same. Stick with the old standards:

1 Ball played just inside left heel.
2 Hands directly above the ball.
3 Feet dug in for balance, even weight distribution.

SHOT RECIPE	
CLUB	Sand wedge
AIM	At target
STANCE	Standard
BALL POSITION	Standard
SWING	Fast (fluffy sand); slower (thin)
FEEL	Match swing length to sand

SHOT 59

Blast From Wet Sand

When the sand gets wet, it gets heavy. Here's how to adjust your swing to splash it like it's dry.

The Situation

It's been raining but that hasn't stopped you from playing the game you love. You hit your approach shot into a greenside bunker and find that the ball is sitting in wet sand.

The Solution

Your goal on this shot is to slide your club under the ball on an angle of approach that will allow for the clubhead to reach its lowest point just in front of the ball. The club never touches the ball, only the sand. But be careful! Wet sand is heavy, so make sure you don't decelerate after impact.

How to Hit It

Like most specialty shots, the secret to pulling it off is in your setup. Copy the positions at right to blast away from a wet sandy lie.

DIFFICULTY LEVEL

| 0 | 1 | 2 | 3 | 4 | 5 |

Swing your club too steep and you'll get stuck in the sand with the ball still in the bunker. Swing your club too shallow and you'll bounce into the ball for an ugly skulked shot.

ACCELERATE
- Wet sand is much heavier than dry sand, meaning you need more speed to move the ball the distance you need.
- The sand will try to stop your swing at impact, making it important to accelerate into a full finish.

Take your lob wedge because it has less bounce at the bottom of the club. In this instance, the increased bounce of your sand wedge will "bounce" your clubhead right into the back of the ball.

CLUB CHOICE
- Bounce is good in dry sand, but not when it's wet. If both your lob and sand wedges feature a lot of bounce, then drop down to your pitching wedge.

SPREAD 'EM
Set up with a wide stance. You'll need a solid foundation to generate necessary clubhead speed.

SHOT RECIPE	
CLUB	Lob wedge
AIM	Left of target
STANCE	Wide and slightly open
BALL POSITION	Center
SWING	From ¾ back to full finish
FEEL	Accelerate though impact

112

OPEN WAY UP
- Set up with the ball in the center of your stance.
- Open your stance so that your hips and shoulders point at least 30 degrees left of your target.
- Rotate the club to the right so that the face is wide open.

STRIKE ANGLE
- Lean the shaft forward and visualize that same lean later at impact to promote a downward blow.

WIDE STANCE
- Take a wider stance so that the insides of your heels are in line with the outsides of your shoulders.

KEY MOVE

IMPACT
- One key to this shot is to maintain your balance, so make a shorter backswing, between halfway to three-quarter back.
- Smoothly accelerate through impact. The sand will be heavy—turn your body as you swing your arms to a full finish.

The Rules Guy

Shotmaking by the Book

"Hey, Ranger– there's water in my bunker!"

Even if it isn't raining, the ball may come to rest in a puddle of water at the base of the bunker. The water may be left over from a previous rain or a busted sprinkler. If the bunker is not completely covered in casual water (not water that's relaxed and informal but rather water that's temporary), you can play your ball as it lies or you can lift and drop it within a club length of the nearest point of relief—without penalty!—as long as you drop in the bunker and not closer to the hole.

If complete relief is not possible, you can drop at the point of maximum available relief, but you still must drop inside the bunker and no closer to the hole. If you decide to drop outside the bunker, that's a one-stroke penalty and you must drop behind the bunker on an imaginary line that runs through the hole and your original lie in the bunker. If the bunker is completely covered in casual water, the same rules are in effect.

In all cases when your ball is in casual water in a bunker you have the option here of deeming your ball unplayable (and when was the last time you got to "deem" anything?) and play a ball from the spot you made the shot that left you in the bunker (with a one-stroke penalty, of course).

113

SHOT

60

Blast From a Bunker Upslope

This shot will fly high and stop softly, so plan accordingly

114

The Situation

Your ball is on the upslope of a bunker. If the pin is close, this lie is an advantage since the ball will fly extra high and land quickly. But if you're hitting to a far pin or into the wind, this becomes a much more difficult shot.

The Solution

The key to hitting this shot is to get your body on the same angle as the incline of the bunker by aligning your shoulders with the slope. Most people don't adjust to the lie and either stick the clubhead in the sand or hit the ball first and fly it over the green.

DIFFICULTY LEVEL

0	1	2	3	4	5

This shot becomes more difficult as the pin gets farther away from you.

STAY BACK
- Focus on keeping your head behind the ball on this shot. This will help you swing with the slope and not jam the club into the face of the bunker.

SUPPORT POST
- Dig your right foot in a little deeper so you can set your weight back and swing up the slope.

TILT IT

- At address, set your right shoulder lower than your left so that your body matches the slope you're standing on.

SHOT RECIPE	
CLUB	Sand wedge
AIM	At target
STANCE	Open; match slope of bunker
BALL POSITION	Slightly forward
SWING	Full backswing to full finish
FEEL	Hit up the slope

Don't Do This

You'll bury the ball in the face of the bunker if you set up with your weight over your left foot or with level shoulders.

HOW TO EXPLODE ON AN UPSLOPE

Step 1

Use your 56-degree wedge since the slope will add loft to this shot. With a 60-degree wedge, this ball will go straight up and you might leave it in the bunker.

Step 2

Set up with the ball slightly forward of center and your stance a little open (toe line pointing to the left of your target). This is where you want to make sure your shoulders are aligned with the slope. Check that your right shoulder sits below your left the same amount your right foot sits below your left foot.

KEY MOVE

Step 3

Because the ball will hit the green and stop with very little roll, **you need to take a full swing** and make sure the ball can fly all the way to the hole. It's easy to stop your swing at impact because of the slope, so try to hang back on your right side a little longer so your wedge glides through the sand and up the hill.

115

SHOT

61

Blast From a Bunker Downslope

Swing "high-to-low" to beat the toughest bunker lie of them all

The Situation
Your ball has come to rest on a downslope in the bunker.

The Solution
Make a "high-to-low" bunker swing, i.e. one that starts at a high position in your backswing and finishes much lower than normal. *Follow the steps at right.*

SHOT RECIPE	
CLUB	Sand wedge
AIM	At target
STANCE	Left foot dug in more
BALL POSITION	Off right heel
SWING	Half-back to half-through
FEEL	Swing down the slope

DIFFICULTY LEVEL

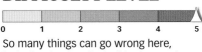

0   1   2   3   4   5

So many things can go wrong here, including leaving the ball in the sand.

EXTRA CARRY
- The downslope portion of the bunker (relative to your stance when you aim at the green) is on the far side of the hazard, so there's a lot of sand to cover.
- If you don't catch this one just right, you'll be hitting your next shot from the sand, too.

LOSS LOFT
- The downslope takes loft off your club, making it difficult to hit the ball on a high, soft trajectory.
- As a result, expect the ball to come out lower and with less spin than if you were on a level lie (Plan for the extra roll once it hits).

116

HOW TO GET THE BALL UP FROM A DOWNHILL BUNKER LIE

KEY MOVE

Keep your hands low in your follow-through.

117

Step 1

Set your address position

• Like you do on all sloping lies, tilt your shoulders and hips to match the slope. If you do it correctly, your left shoulder will sit below your right shoulder the same amount that your left foot sits below your right foot.

• Since the sand behind the ball is higher than the sand in front of the ball, play the ball way back in your stance.

• Dig your left foot deeper into the sand than your right for extra support.

Step 2

Swing back high

• Take the club back with mostly your arms (notice how little the legs move in the backswing). Add to your arm swing a significant amount of wrist hinge.

• Think about pointing the butt of your sand wedge at the ball as you hinge the club up.

Step 3

Swing through low

Enter the sand about an inch behind the ball. Since the ball is positioned back in your stance, your downswing will be fairly steep.

• Once your club makes contact with the sand, swing down the slope and keep your hands low to the ground all the way into your follow-through.

• Turn through the shot with your upper body (try to point your chest at the target at your finish). This makes it difficult to leave your club in the sand and hit the shot too short.

LOW POINTS

• The secret to this shot is swinging down the slope after impact.

• Keep your hands and clubhead low to the ground in your follow-through.

F.Y.I.
In a recent survey of 200 golfers just like you, the downhill bunker blast was rated the most difficult shot in golf.

SHOT

62 Ball Above Your Feet

The trick here is not to take too much sand

118

STAND TALL

- Since the ball is closer to you, stand erect. A straight spine automatically makes your swing flatter—perfect for this situation.

CHEST GAME

- To make sure you enter the sand at the right spot and take the right-sized divot, play the ball under the logo of your shirt and aim for a spot in the sand directly under your sternum.

AIM HERE

- Like any shot where the ball is above your feet, this one is going to hook left on you. Play the ball right of the flag and let it curl to the cup.

DIFFICULTY LEVEL

0   1   2   3   4   5

It's a challenge to take the right amount of sand from an uneven lie in the bunker, and this is no exception.

The Situation

Your approach finds the upslope of a greenside bunker. Your lie is good, but when you go to take your stance the ball is way above your feet.

The Solution

With the ball so close to you, the bottom of your natural swing arc occurs too far underneath the ball—you'll take too much sand and likely leave the ball in the bunker. To guard against this, shorten your club by standing tall and choking down on the grip at least two inches. Other than that, make your normal, everyday bunker swing.

SHOT RECIPE	
CLUB	Sand wedge
AIM	Way right of target
STANCE	Square to aim line
BALL POSITION	Under logo of shirt
SWING	Full bunker motion
FEEL	Swing around your spine

HOW TO BLAST IT FROM A SIDEHILL

Step 1

Copy these setup positions:

1. Choke down on the grip to make the club shorter so you don't dig too far deep into the sand—the common mistake here.
2. Stand erect with your spine nearly straight up-and-down.
3. Play the ball off the logo of your shirt (just slightly inside your left heel).
4. Dig in with your feet for balance. The more you dig in, the more you should choke down on the club. (Digging in lowers the spot where your swing bottoms out.)
5. Aim right of the hole—this ball will go left.

Step 2

If you make a steep swing *[dotted line]*, you'll bury the club in the hill and the ball will go nowhere. But instead of thinking about making a flatter swing, just take the club back. The reason behind this is that your swing naturally moves around your spine, and if your spine is straight up-and-down, your swing will flatten out by itself.

Step 3

Copy the picture at left and explode into the sand at a point directly underneath your chest. The explosion will carry the ball out and onto the green. Once the ball hits it will roll left because of the automatic sidespin created by a sidehill lie.

KEY MOVE

Blasting from a bunker with the ball above your feet requires a unique setup.

CHECK!
Make sure you hit the easiest shot. If you played at the flag here, you'd have a downhill lie with the ball above your feet. Ouch.

119

SHOT 63 Ball Below Your Feet

Your knees are the key to digging the ball out and getting it up and on

The Situation

You cut your approach shot and found the right-hand side of a bunker on the right side of the green. Not only do you have to stand outside the bunker to take your normal stance, the ball is miles below your feet.

The Solution

You have a hard time staying down on the ball on regular full swings, so how are you going to do it here? That's a good question to ask your knees, since you'll need to bend them at address in order to get your club down to the ball. More important, they'll have to remain bent during your swing or you'll leave a gash on the top half of the ball. Control your knees and this becomes a relatively simple bunker shot.

WIDE STANCE

- Standing with your feet wider apart gives you a more solid base from which to swing and drops your club closer to the ball.

FLEX APPEAL

- Flex your knees at address and keep them flexed during your swing.
- As soon as your knees straighten, the odds of you making solid contact plummet.

DIFFICULTY LEVEL

| 0 | 1 | 2 | 3 | 4 | 5 |

Catching it thin or whiffing completely are real possibilities. Plus, your caddy may have to lift you out if you tumble forward into the bunker.

DIG DOWN

- Come down sharply into the sand behind the ball.
- This is a good mental image because the last thing you want is to come in flat.
- A flat swing when the ball is below your feet will likely result in a skull.

SHOT RECIPE	
CLUB	Sand wedge
AIM	Slightly left of target
STANCE	Square to aim line
BALL POSITION	Under logo of shirt
SWING	Full bunker motion
FEEL	Keep your knees flexed

HOW TO ESCAPE THE SAND WHEN THE BALL IS BELOW YOUR FEET

Step 1

Pick a spot
Like any bunker shot, take care selecting your landing area. (This is a hard shot, but you should still plan to land the ball exactly where you want.) The ball is going to trickle right from this lie, so play left of the pin.

Step 2

Hunker down
It's going to take some effort to get it all the way down to the ball. Set the ball off the logo of your shirt and then...

1 Take a wider stance.
2 Bend from your hips until your back is nearly parallel to the ground.
3 Flex your knees.

These three setup moves combine to "lengthen" your club and move the bottom of your swing arc below the ball.

Step 3

Get steep
With a flat spine your swing automatically gets steep, so you don't have to think about moving the club way above plane—just take it back and through like a normal sand shot.

KEY MOVE

Drop to your knees when the ball is *waaay* below your feet

If the ball is so far below your feet you fear you'll split your khakis right where the sun don't shine trying to bend down to the ball, try hitting the shot from your knees. You may have never thought to take a swipe from your knees, but dropping down to this stance gives you plenty of room to swing your arms through the hitting zone—always a must. It also allows you to set the club at its natural lie angle (or close to it). The only penalty is an extra trip to the dry cleaners.

How to do it

Your knees and shins give you plenty of ground support, so don't be afraid to make an aggressive swing (flare both feet out for an even wider base). **Keep your rear end and your back straight, and hold this position as you swing the club back and through.** Don't pick the club up—get your shoulders moving as well as your arms.

The biggest mistake you can make is bending over too much. That makes it easy to lose your balance. Use your butt as ballast to keep your posture tall and your swing in control.

If the ball is so far below your feet that your bent legs don't give your arms any room to swing back to impact, then play the shot from your knees.

121

SHOT

64
Against the Lip

Don't kiss off a par save just yet—this bunker-beater works like a charm

The Situation
Your ball is up against the lip of a steep bunker and you have to get it up quick and carry it 10 yards.

The Solution
In this situation, your angle of attack needs to be very shallow. Too steep an approach will drive the ball into the bank. Here's how to add loft with a flatter swing.

122

SHOT RECIPE	
CLUB	Lob wedge
AIM	Left of target
STANCE	Open, weight over left foot
BALL POSITION	Slightly right of center
SWING	Full to impact then stop
FEEL	A shallow downswing

DIFFICULTY LEVEL

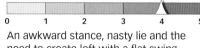

0   1   2   3   4   5

An awkward stance, nasty lie and the need to create loft with a flat swing make this shot especially tough.

BRACE HERE
- Your left leg will be your support leg for this shot.

OPEN HERE
- You'll need at least 90 degrees of loft to pull off this shot.
- Lay your lob wedge wide open.

HOW TO BUST ONE FROM THE LIP

Shoulders match slope.

Step 1

Open the clubface
You need the ball to climb straight up in the air, which requires about 90 degrees of loft. If you have a lob wedge, use it.
Key adjustment: Lay the face wide open so the grooves point straight at the sky [photo below]. Brace yourself against the hill with your left leg and set your hips and shoulders parallel to the slope. Your hands should be behind the ball, so that the shaft angles slightly away from the slope.

Wide-open clubface.

Roll your forearms.

Slide club under ball.

SKIP IT HERE

On your forward-swing, pretend you're skipping a stone across the water with your right arm. You'll keep your right arm underneath your left and your right palm and clubface pointed skyward, maximizing loft through the shot.

ALTERNATIVE METHODS

"Hit and Recoil" to Escape the Lip

If the lip is severe—or your wrists can't handle a collision—try this

Normally, you can loft the ball high out of the sand by opening your clubface and swinging sharply down. But in this instance, you're going to endure some wrist pain with this move because you're bound to slam into the lip. Unless you add the following wrinkle:

As you swing down, prepare to pull the club back as soon as you make contact. This isn't as difficult as it sounds. Just start your pull-back motion as soon as your clubhead reaches the midpoint of your downswing. You won't affect your downward thrust, and as soon as the club enters the sand it will yank back easily. The trick is to pull back with your elbows and forearms, not your hands and wrists. Your elbows and forearms are attached to much stronger muscles than those that control your hands and wrists. It's the same move major league batters make when they check their swings.

Practice this move a few times before you do it for real. If you keep your clubface sufficiently open, the ball will pop almost straight up and land soft. The further the distance the ball must carry, the harder you must swing.

123

Step 2

Roll your forearms
Unlike a plugged lie, your attack angle here is shallow. Too steep an approach will drive the ball into the bank.
Key image: As you take the club back, roll your hands and forearms to the inside [photo below], as if you were trying to wrap the club around your body. Make a full shoulder turn—with so much loft, you're going to need twice the normal clubhead speed to get the carry you want.

Step 3

Let go
Slide the clubhead underneath the ball, leading with the heel so it enters the sand before the toe.
Key moment: As the club enters the sand, allow your right hand to come off the club slightly [photo below]. This will soften the blow to your right wrist as the club slams into the bank, diminishing the chance of injury. It also ensures that the face remains open, projecting the ball straight up.

After impact [below], pull the club back [left]. The "hit and recoil" is a great lip-beater.

An inside takeaway.

Right hand lets go.

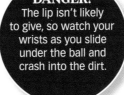

DANGER!
The lip isn't likely to give, so watch your wrists as you slide under the ball and crash into the dirt.

SHOT

65
Flop From the Sand

This extra-high, extra-soft sand shot will leave you close from ultra-short range

124

What It Is
The bunker version of a flop shot—the ball goes high and not very far.

When to Use It
When you're in the bunker with a decent lie and there's little room between you and the pin.

How to Hit It
Normally you'd open the face of your sand wedge, open your stance and cut across the ball to hit it high out of a bunker. But in extremes situations like this, a simple cut shot won't get the job done, so follow these steps to really launch the ball high and land it softly next to the pin.

DIFFICULTY LEVEL

| 0 | 1 | 2 | 3 | 4 | 5 |

You'll need to practice this shot to time the way you flip the clubhead past your hands at the bottom of your swing. If you take too much sand during your practice, dig in less with your feet.

BREAK AWAY
- For this shot you'll break one of the game's most rock-solid fundamentals— letting the clubhead pass your hands.
- In this situation, however, it gives your shot extra loft from the sand you can't get from the standard technique.

FLIP IT
- Flip the clubhead past your hands though impact (but make sure your right hand stays under your left).

TAKE SAND
- Even though this is a specialty sand shot, the old rule applies: The ball flies out on a cushion of sand.

F.Y.I.
The flop-from-the-sand technique also works when you have a fluffy lie in the rough, but don't try it from tight fairway lies.

HOW TO LOFT A SAND SHOT

Plan to enter the sand here.

Step 1

Use your lob wedge and set up square to your target with the clubface pointing exactly where you want the ball to land. Play the ball almost off your left heel, and tilt your upper body away from the target.

Step 2

Aim for a spot an inch behind the ball, and as you enter the sand, keep your weight back and allow the club to pass your hands [photo, left]. It should feel like you're slapping the bottom of the club against the sand under the ball.

Keep your right hand under your left as you make the slap move through impact.

DON'T DO THIS

As you flip the clubhead past your hands, don't slap it to the left [photo, below]. Your right hand should flip under your left hand so that the clubface points straight up in your follow-through, not behind you [photo, left].

SHOT RECIPE	
CLUB	Lob wedge
AIM	At target
STANCE	Square to target
BALL POSITION	Off left heel
SWING	½ backswing, ¾ finish
FEEL	Club passes hands at impact

125

66

40-Yard Sand Shot

Learn two plays to double your chances of knocking it stiff from an all-time tough lie

The Situation

You laid an acre of sod over the ball on your approach and came up woefully short of your target. Not only that, the ball ended up in a bunker and now you're faced with a 40-yard sand shot to the green. On Tour, players get up-and-down from this position only 30% of the time.

The Solution

This shot leaves most golfers quivering in their spikes. You rarely get the opportunity to practice a 40-yard bunker blast, so when you step in the sand you feel a little lost. However, you already own the tools needed to turn this deadly scenario into a great par save. Either turn up the heat on your regular bunker-blast technique or pick it clean like a pitch shot. Here's how to decide between each option and knock this ball stiff.

126

DIFFICULTY LEVEL

| 0 | 1 | 2 | 3 | 4 | 5 |

Catch too much sand and you'll be left with a 30-yard bunker shot. Catch the ball on the thin side and it'll sail over the green.

KEY MOVE

To pick it, enter the sand *in front of* the ball. Swing your clubhead into the sand behind the ball to blast it.

KNEE HIGH

- If you opt to pick the ball, make a knee-high to knee-high swing with your pitching wedge. That's plenty of power to knock the ball on the green from 40 yards.

CHECK!
You'll consistently generate more distance with the pick technique, so if there's trouble short, it's the automatic play.

LIP CHECK

- If you're in a steep bunker with a big lip, go with the blast technique. If the bunker is shallow like it is here, opt for the pick shot.

CRITIC'S PICK

- You may never have though to pick the ball clean from this lie, but it's a great option if you often leave long sand shots short.

SHOT RECIPE	
CLUB	SW (blast); PW (pick)
AIM	Slightly left of target
STANCE	Standard (but don't dig in)
BALL POSITION	Left heel (blast); left thigh (pick)
SWING	¾ (blast); knee-high (pick)
FEEL	Hit before ball (blast); after (pick)

BLAST THE BALL IF...

- The sand isn't too firm or too fluffy.
- At least a quarter of your ball is buried.
- The lip facing you is above waist height.

HOW TO DO IT

- Use your **sand wedge** and take your normal bunker setup with the ball played off your left heel, but don't dig your feet in.
- If your full sand-wedge distance from the fairway is 80 yards, expect to generate about 60 yards from this setup. Therefore, make a slightly less-than-full swing.
- Enter the sand about two inches behind the ball and swing to a full finish.

When blasting the ball, play it off your left heel but don't dig your feet in.

PICK THE BALL IF...

- The sand is firm or fluffy.
- Your ball is sitting up.
- The bunker is shallow.

HOW TO DO IT

- Use your **pitching wedge** and play the ball just inside your left thigh.
- Don't dig in with your feet. Your goal is to contact the ball first and the sand second. This is a lot easier to do if you forward-press your hands at address.
- Keep your lower body quiet and swing knee-high to knee-high. Add just a touch of wrist hinge on your backswing, but make sure your left wrist is flat at impact.

Hit the ball first then enter the sand when trying to pick it from 40 yards.

127

SHOT

67

Approach From a Fairway Bunker

Stop treating this shot like it's a rescue shot

128

The Situation
You just missed your target off the tee and the ball rolled into a fairway bunker. The lie is perfect, you have a clear line to the flagstick and you're only 160 yards from the green—a 7-iron for you from a fairway lie.

The Solution
Change the way you think about fairway bunkers. They're not penalty areas (what most golfers see them as just because they're filled with sand). The truth is that a fairway bunker is a fairly easy place to hit from, especially if the ball is up. The following setup and swing adjustments are minor compared to the ones you need from greenside bunkers. There's no reason why you can't knock this one on.

MAKE ROOM
- You're used to making swings from a bunker with a shorter club. Here you'll be using something longer, so make sure to keep your distance from the ball.
- Aim slightly left and play a fade. A little cut swing will help you pick it cleanly off the sand.

SHORT CLUB
- Stand taller, don't dig your feet in the sand and choke down on the grip.
- This allows you to make a fairly standard swing and catch the ball on its equator without digging up lots of sand.

DIFFICULTY LEVEL

0   1   2   3   4

Think of this shot as an easy three-quarter swing with more arm action than lower-body action. Take an extra club and you'll get on more often than not.

HOW TO HIT IT ON FROM A FAIRWAY BUNKER

Step 1

This is an important first step. When you step into the sand, don't dig your feet in like you do in a greenside bunker. You want to keep the bottom of your swing arc at the level of the sand. Some light shuffling is all you need.

Step 2

Position the ball a hair back of where you normally play it with the club in your hands. Speaking of clubs, take an extra one and choke down on it about an inch. The reason you're taking an extra club is because you're choking down on it, and you need the choke so you ensure that you don't hit too far under the ball.

Step 3

Take the club back like you usually do (it helps to swing a little steeper, but don't overdo it). Make a smooth, three-quarter move so you don't sway in your stance. Remember, your feet are just resting on the surface of the sand.

KEY MOVE

Step 4

Come down as smoothly as you went back. Feel like you're standing taller through impact [photo, left], leaving room for your club to swing under you and pick the ball off the turf. (You should take a little sand after impact).

Step 5

Swing to a full finish with your chest and hips facing the target. You know you've done it right if you finish in balance and your left foot hasn't spun out. That means you properly took your legs out of the swing and turned through with your upper body—a great way to pick the ball off any surface.

NO PENALTY

- If your lie is good, make the flagstick your target.
- A fairway bunker shot is not a trouble shot. With the right swing you'll get almost the full distance of the club.

SHOT RECIPE	
CLUB	One more than the distance
AIM	Slightly left
STANCE	Don't dig feet in
BALL POSITION	Center
SWING	¾-backswing to full finish
FEEL	Quiet legs on downswing

The Rules Guy

Shotmaking by the Book

Avoid an Identity Crisis In the Bunker

When the ball rolls into a fairway bunker, you're usually left with a decent to good lie. When it plugs after traveling 230 yards at 110 mph, your lie can be downright nasty, especially if the sand is soft or the ball strikes an upslope. Sometimes, the ball plain disappears. Other times only a fraction of the ball is visible in the sand.

In these situations, it's important that you identify your ball—you don't want to incur a penalty for hitting the wrong Titleist. **You're allowed to probe the sand with your fingers or your club until you can locate the identifying mark on your ball.** In the event you move the ball, a simple "oops" will do. Just replace it and, if necessary, re-cover it to establish the original lie. No penalty.

If identifying your ball means you have to lift it from the bunker, you may lift it without penalty. Before you lift, however, you must announce your intention to your opponent in match play or a fellow-competitor in stroke play and mark the position of the ball. You can then lift the ball and identify it, provided that you allow your competitor an opportunity to observe the lifting and replacement (we're sure they'll be *rivited*). Just make sure you don't clean the ball while it's in your hands. This one deserves to stay dirty.

129

Around The
Green

6

Greenside Super-Shots

The ball can bury itself, but it can't hide, especially when you know how to get up-and-down from anywhere around the green

WHEN YOU MISS A GREEN you usually don't end up in a nice patch of fairway grass, even if you erred by only a few feet. That's because most putting surfaces are guarded tighter than Fort Knox, with deep grass, waste areas and cavernous hollows offering a formidable defense. In some situations, your normal pitch and chip techniques don't stand a chance against these tough greenside lies. (You know you've been in one if you've skulled the ball into a bunker on the other side of the green with what you thought was a perfectly executed shot.) Here you're forced to be at your creative best, but before you doff your thinking cap, try the following greenside super-shots on for size. They'll get you closer to the pin than your old pitches and chips ever could.

68 How to Hit a Lengthy Pitch

This special knockdown play gets you close from 30 to 50 yards out

The Situation
The pin is all the way back on a long par 5, and two solid shots have left you 50 yards out—in position to make birdie.

The Solution
You could try flying the ball to the hole, but why not take advantage of all that green? A shot that flies lower and runs more is easier to execute than a high ball. Call it the "knockdown pitch."

HOW TO HIT A KNOCKDOWN PITCH

Step 1
Grab a 9-iron and take a narrow, slightly open stance with the ball just back of center and your weight favoring your left side. Press your hands toward the target slightly to de-loft the clubface.

Step 2
Make an abbreviated swing controlled almost entirely by your arms. Don't consciously hinge your wrists going back.

DANGER!
It's easy to hood the clubhead with this short swing, causing heavy shots. Rotate the face open as you take the club back.

SET UP
- Address the ball with your hands forward, ball back and weight favoring your left side.

DIFFICULTY LEVEL

0	1	2	3	4	5

Don't expect to hit this one pure at the start. You'll need practice to learn the right arm action and to produce consistent distances.

SHOT RECIPE	
CLUB	9-iron
AIM	Left of target
STANCE	Narrow
BALL POSITION	Slightly back of center
SWING	Half back to half through
FEEL	Pull down with your left arm

132

Step 3

Coming down, pull the club through impact with your left arm. The club should thud against the ground, resulting in a low finish. The ball will bounce hard a couple of times and then roll like a putt.

- While the knockdown is easy to control for overall distance, it's difficult to be precise on the carry distance.
- If there is deep rough or a hazard near your landing spot, consider a normal, high-trajectory pitch that takes the obstacles out of play.

SHOT

69
Chip Over a Bunker

Hit down to get over any obstacle standing between you and the pin

The Situation

You have 20 yards to the hole, but there's a bunker (or water, or a bush) in between.

The Solution

This appears to be a tricky situation, but it's not. All of your wedges have enough loft to carry the bunker, so you don't need to scoop, flop or lift the ball into the air. Plus, these are risky plays that pay off only once in a while. Just focus on making solid contact and actually hitting the ball low and you'll end up in perfect shape.

How to Chip It Over and Close

Set up with the ball positioned in the middle of your stance, then lean your body toward the target so that your head is slightly in front of the ball. This sets you up to come down sharply into impact. While you may think hitting down creates a low shot, it's actually what gets the ball into the air. If your impact position looks like the photo at right, the ball will fly high and land soft.

DIFFICULTY LEVEL

0   1   2   3   4   5

This is one of the most straightforward short-game shots you'll face.

HANDS
Swing them toward the target and you might shank it. Instead, move them to the left of your target after impact.

EYES
Maintain focus on the ball, not where it's going. If you peek, your contact will suffer.

ARMS
Keep them loose and feel as if they're extending as you swing through impact.

KEY MOVE

Make sure that the clubhead never gets higher than your hands. At the finish, your hands should be at hip height with the clubhead hovering near your left knee.

CLUBHEAD
Try to brush the grass in front of the ball— it's an easy way to stop thin and fat contact.

FEET
Close together so you stand a little taller at address.

SHOT RECIPE	
CLUB	Any wedge
AIM	At target
STANCE	Narrow
BALL POSITION	Center
SWING	Half back to half through
FEEL	Swinging left of target

133

SHOT 70
One-Hop-and-Stop Pitch

This shot lands close then bites harder than a miner's handshake

What It Is
A crisp pitch shot that hits the green, takes one hop forward and then stops because it's spinning faster than a top on steroids.

When to Use It
From a good lie in the fairway when you have about 30 yards to the green. The pin is cut in the front—if you hit a normal pitch the ball will hit the green and run past the hole. You need this thing to land and then stop.

How to Hit It
To stop the ball like you want you'll need clubhead speed and a trapping type of impact, where the club literally pinches the ball against the turf. Most recreational players have difficulty trapping the ball on full swings. The trick is to take a stance that makes it happen automatically. *Follow the steps at right:*

DIFFICULTY LEVEL

| 0 | 1 | 2 | 3 | 4 | 5 |

It's an awkward stance and the type of contact you need isn't what you normally produce. Practice this one on the range a few times before pulling it out on the course.

TRAP ACTION
- You get extra spin when you trap the ball against the turf at impact. Scoopy impact gives you a knuckleball.

WEIGHT LEFT
- Set up with your right foot pulled back. This will help you keep your weight forward so you can properly hit down on the ball.

134

LANDING PAD
- Since the ball is going to stop once it hits, pick an aggressive landing spot and leave yourself an easy chance at birdie.

ARC STUDY
- Even though you're hitting sand wedge, don't expect much height on this shot.
- The ball should travel on a slight arc—if you hit a lobber you didn't trap the ball and you won't get the spin you need.

SHOT RECIPE	
CLUB	Sand wedge
AIM	At target
STANCE	Weight forward
BALL POSITION	Off left foot
SWING	Half-backswing to half finish
FEEL	"Pinch" the ball

HOW TO STOP THE BALL ON A DIME

Open the face just a few degrees.

Step 1

Grab your sand wedge and open the face a few degrees—you're going to swing fast here so you need extra loft or the ball will carry too far.

Pull your right foot back and set your weight left.

Step 2

Play the ball off your left foot and shift all of your weight forward. This makes it easier to hit down on the ball and trap it against the turf. To make sure your weight stays forward, pull your right foot back. From here, make an abbreviated backswing (hands to about hip height) and keep your weight over your left leg.

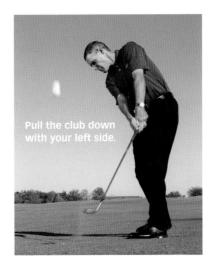

Pull the club down with your left side.

Step 3

On your downswing, move the club with your body as well as your hands—like your whole left side is pulling the club down and into the back of the ball. This is not a shot you're trying to pick clean. Accelerate through the ball and dig up some turf.

KEY MOVE

Finish left of the target.

Step 4

Keep accelerating through impact and swing left of the target on your follow-through. Since all you're trying to do is trap the ball, cut your finish when your hands reach about hip height. You know you did it right if your clubhead and chest point left of the target.

135

SHOT

71 Classic Bump-and-Run

Ditch your pitch for one of the game's all-time great short-game shots

What It Is
A specialty pitch that travels in the air a few yards (the bump) and then scampers along the ground to your target (the run).

When to Use It
You've left your second shot short of the green—about 30 yards short—and there's nothing between you and the pin but grass. Or, you face an uphill chip to a pin that's cut on the back tier of a multilevel green.

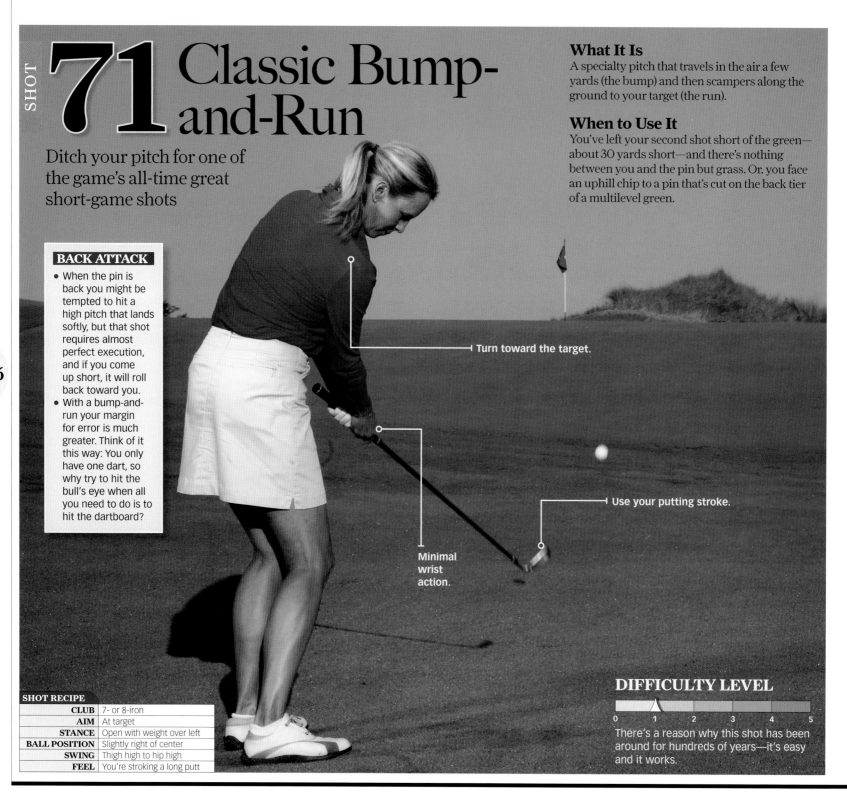

BACK ATTACK
- When the pin is back you might be tempted to hit a high pitch that lands softly, but that shot requires almost perfect execution, and if you come up short, it will roll back toward you.
- With a bump-and-run your margin for error is much greater. Think of it this way: You only have one dart, so why try to hit the bull's eye when all you need to do is to hit the dartboard?

Turn toward the target.

Use your putting stroke.

Minimal wrist action.

136

SHOT RECIPE	
CLUB	7- or 8-iron
AIM	At target
STANCE	Open with weight over left
BALL POSITION	Slightly right of center
SWING	Thigh high to hip high
FEEL	You're stroking a long putt

DIFFICULTY LEVEL

0 1 2 3 4 5

There's a reason why this shot has been around for hundreds of years—it's easy and it works.

HOW TO BUMP IT CLOSE

Step 1

Select your 7- or 8-iron to keep the shot low, and set up with the ball slightly right of center. The club should feel like an extension of your left arm, with your right arm bisecting the two.

Stand closer with your 8- or 7-iron so it sits like your putter.

Step 2

Use a pendulum motion with minimal wrist action—like you're hitting a long putt. If you feel you need to take your hands back farther than thigh height, use a longer club.

Add a bit of wrist hinge to get some pop on the ball.

Step 3

Turn through the shot like normal, but use the same arm, shoulder and hand action you'd use for a long putt.

CHECK!
On a standard bump-and-run, the ball will run 8 to 10 times farther than the bump, so take care picking the right landing spot.

KEY MOVE Treat this shot like a long putt with a turn toward the target.

Chip with your hybrid from long distance

The longer shaft gives you more distance with a smaller motion

Move your knees slightly toward the target for a more fluid motion and crisper contact.

Hybrids have long been considered useful alternatives to long irons, but in some situations—like when you're faced with a long chip from a tight lie—they outperform even your trusty wedge. The extra weight and longer shaft length of a hybrid allow you to make a smooth, short stroke and still create a lot of distance. Even from distances as far as 100 feet, you have plenty of club in your hands to roll the ball close, so all you need to do is concentrate on making your normal putting stroke (very similar to the technique you learned on the opposite page). Practice, however, is recommended to develop distance control and touch.

Play the ball directly under your right eye and grip down an inch on the handle to add more wrist movement to your stroke. Narrow your stance (heels just inside your shoulders) and set your weight slightly forward. As you sole your club on the ground and set the face square to your target line, flex your knees—you're going to need them on your downswing (so don't lock them, either).

As you take the club away, swing the triangle formed by your arms and shoulders in a pendulum motion.

Try to keep your lower body quiet and add a little wrist motion for a touch of feel.

On your forwardswing, unhinge your wrists—put back what you took out—and accelerate. Add just a touch of forward knee movement. This will make your motion a lot more fluid and keep you from jabbing at the ball. In fact, you shouldn't even think about your strike—simply let the ball get in the way of your stroke.

137

SHOT

72 Pitch From the Short Side

Locate the pin and use one of these three plays to take the guesswork out of pitching

The Situation

Your approach missed short and slightly to the right or left of the green. In golf terms, you "short-sided" your approach. There's about 20 yards between you and the center of the putting surface, your lie is good and your path is clear.

The Solution

You're tempted to grab your sand wedge and make a long backswing if the pin is back and a short backswing if it's up. But how short is short? And how long is long? Guess wrong and you could end up miles from the hole—and that will cost you strokes. Each of the three possible pin positions

VARIETY PACK

- You shouldn't swing harder if the pin is back or slower if the pin is up. Changing tempo like this is the quick way to hit a grounder instead of a crisp pitch.
- Match the club and wrist action to the pin location using the clues on these pages and apply the same speed to make pitching from the short side a piece of cake.

FRONT PIN

Club: Lob wedge.
Ball position: Off right foot.
Weight: Over left foot.
- Don't try to lob the ball into the air. That takes perfect execution. Plan for a low shot (which is why the ball is off your right foot) but use your lob wedge. It will give you just enough height to stop the ball close.
Key move: Keep your wrists quiet and make a simple pendulum stroke back and through with your arms, like you would on a long putt.

SHOT RECIPE	
CLUB	SW, GW or LW
AIM	At target
STANCE	Standard pitch stance
BALL POSITION	Depends on pin position
SWING	Putt stroke with/without hinge
FEEL	See wrist action notes

(back, middle and front) requires a distinct amount of loft, spin and carry if you want to get the ball close. That means learning three specific pitch shots. Luckily, these don't stray very far from your everyday technique.

DIFFICULTY LEVEL

0	1	2	3	4	5

Delicate short shots are tough to master, especially if you use the same swing on every one. Learn to vary the trajectory and this situation won't be as daunting.

✓ **CHECK!**
When the flag is back, take a quick read of the green. The ball will spend more time rolling on the ground than in the air.

MIDDLE PIN

Club: Sand wedge.
Ball position: Middle.
Weight: Even.

• In this situation you want to land the ball on the front third of the green and then let it track to the hole. If you're more comfortable with a gap wedge, that also will work, but a sand wedge gives you a bit more spin to help slow down the roll.

Key move: Take your hands a bit farther back on this swing (past thigh height) but don't break your wrists.

BACK PIN

Club: Gap wedge.
Ball position: Middle.
Weight: Even.

• Land the ball halfway between you and the pin (count on the ball rolling just as far as it flies in the air). If the pin is way back or the green tilts uphill, drop down to a pitching wedge.

Key move: Hinge your wrists so the clubhead is just above your hands. Keep your arms together and your hands ahead of the clubhead all the way into impact.

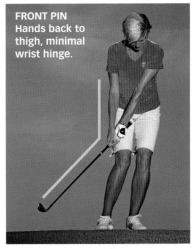

FRONT PIN
Hands back to thigh, minimal wrist hinge.

MIDDLE PIN
Hands past thigh high, but no wrist hinge.

139

BACK PIN
Hinge the clubhead just above your hands.

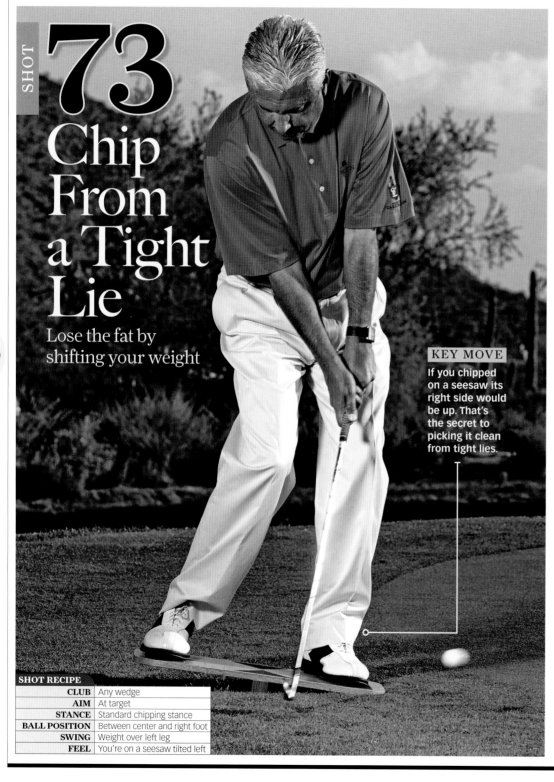

73

Chip From a Tight Lie

Lose the fat by shifting your weight

140

KEY MOVE
If you chipped on a seesaw its right side would be up. That's the secret to picking it clean from tight lies.

SHOT RECIPE	
CLUB	Any wedge
AIM	At target
STANCE	Standard chipping stance
BALL POSITION	Between center and right foot
SWING	Weight over left leg
FEEL	You're on a seesaw tilted left

The Situation

Your ball is lying just off the green on freshly mown fairway. The grass is so tight you could bounce a quarter off it. Some players enjoy ultra-tight lies, but you prefer chipping with a cushion of rough beneath the ball.

The Solution

At address, picture yourself balanced on a small seesaw. At address, the seesaw should tilt to the left. This means your weight is perfectly positioned so you can hit down on the ball and catch it clean.

How to Practice It

Hit chips with an empty plastic water bottle under your right foot [*photo, below right*]. Play the ball slightly back of center, and use the bottle to remind you to shift your weight over to your left leg. Shifting your weight forward and keeping it there during your stroke correctly positions the bottom of your swing arc at the back of the ball—you won't be able to hit the ground behind the ball if you try.

Don't Do This...
Just shifting your hips isn't enough. Your weight remains back (because your torso is leaning away from the target).

Do This...
Keep your weight forward. Place a bottle under your right foot to set your weight left during practice.

DIFFICULTY LEVEL

0   1   2   3   4   5

Solve your weight shift problems with this drill and you'll look forward to playing chips from tight grass.

Lob Wedge vs. Sand Wedge

Match the design trait to the situation at hand for optimal results

Every short-game shot comes with an option: lob wedge or sand wedge. But do you ever really know which of these short-game stalwarts is the right tool for the job at hand? A quick study of their design makes the decision much easier.

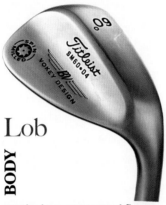

Lob

BODY

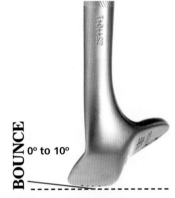

BOUNCE 0° to 10°

FACE

LW The less-pronounced flange on the sole of a lob wedge slips more easily under the ball, which gets the ball up quickly on short, delicate shots to tight pin placements.

LW Zero to 10 degrees of bounce allow a lob wedge to catch the ball cleanly on normal and tight lies.

LW 60 degrees (or more) of loft makes the lob wedge perfect for full-swing shots that fly high and land softly.

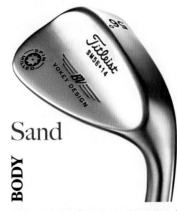

Sand

BODY

BOUNCE 10° to 16°

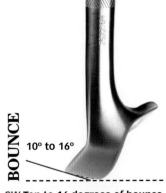

FACE

SW The large flange on the sole of a sand wedge gives the club more momentum to plow through heavy sand or grass.

SW Ten to 16 degrees of bounce keeps your sand wedge from digging into fluffy sand or heavy grass, but can lead to iffy contact from a fairway lie.

SW With 54 to 57 degrees of loft, the sand wedge still gets the ball up, but it allows you to fly your shot to a more distant target.

WHY YOU SHOULD TRY A 64-DEGREE WEDGE

Extra loft made the 60-degree lob wedge a runaway hit. Its creator, *Dave Pelz*, is pushing for even more.

"One of the first things I discovered when I took my research to the Tour was that players needed more loft to combat the speed of modern greens," says *GOLF Magazine*'s technical and short-game consultant, Dave Pelz. "I built my first 60° lob wedge for Tom Kite in 1979. He carried it along with his sand and pitching wedges during the '80 season and quickly became regarded as one of the world's best wedge players." In 1981, Kite captured the Vardon Trophy and the money title—the three-wedge era had officially begun.

Through the 1980s and '90s, Tour greens continued to roll faster. **"My research near the end of the last decade concluded that pros required even more loft to stop the ball quickly,"** says Pelz. "One of the cornerstones of my teaching philosophy has always been that the closer you chip and pitch the ball to the hole, the more putts you'll make. The obvious strategy, then, was to create the 64° X-wedge, which I did and offered to Tour players in the early 2000s."

More than 40 players on Tour now carry four wedges, including Phil Mickelson. "Much has been made of Phil's tendency to carry two drivers, but he also carries four wedges—including an X-wedge—that helps his scoring," says Pelz. "My advice is to follow his lead and give an X-wedge a test run. You don't need to adjust your technique to get the most out of it. Just keep accelerating through impact like you do with any of your wedges and you'll produce the highest, softest shots you've ever hit. They'll stop quickly by the pin, too, giving you the best chance of making your first putt."

141

SHOT

74 Chip From a Downslope

Pull your right foot back to beat this tricky lie

The Situation
Your ball is on a severe downhill lie near the green. You struggle when your left foot is lower than your right on full swings, and feel even more uncomfortable trying to chip from this position.

The Solution
Notice how when you take your normal chipping stance from this lie your right knee blocks the path your hands take back to impact. The trick is to remove the interference caused by your right leg and then make your normal chipping motion. *Here's how:*

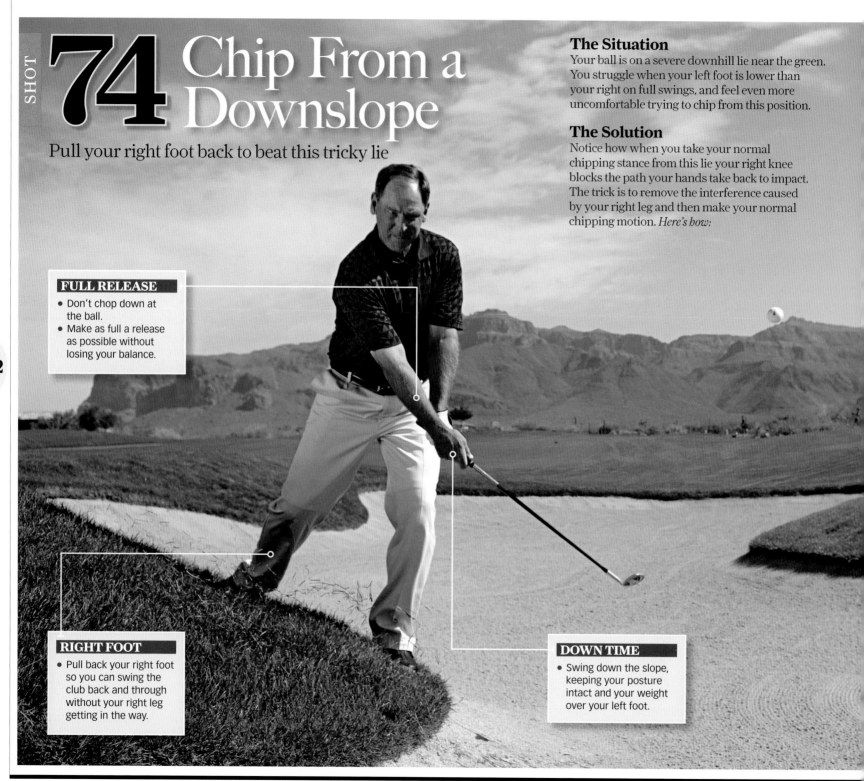

FULL RELEASE
- Don't chop down at the ball.
- Make as full a release as possible without losing your balance.

RIGHT FOOT
- Pull back your right foot so you can swing the club back and through without your right leg getting in the way.

DOWN TIME
- Swing down the slope, keeping your posture intact and your weight over your left foot.

142

DIFFICULTY LEVEL

| 0 | 1 | 2 | 3 | 4 | 5 |

You only need to make one minor adjustment to catch this shot clean. If the slope isn't too severe, your chances of knocking the ball close are very high.

SHOT RECIPE

CLUB	Sand wedge
AIM	At target
STANCE	Right foot pulled back
BALL POSITION	Off right heel
SWING	Along the slope
FEEL	Release the club fully

HOW TO CATCH IT CLEAN FROM A DOWNSLOPE

KEY MOVE

Step 1

Set up with a shoulder-width stance and position the ball just inside your right foot. Tilt your shoulders to the left until they're even with the slope. (You can flare your left foot a little to maintain your balance.)

Step 2

Move your right foot behind you (away from the target line) by about a foot or so. You now have a clear inside-to-out path that the club can follow to the ball.

DON'T DO THIS...
If you don't pull back your right foot, your right leg will block your swing back and down to the ball.

Step 3

Swing back and through along the slope. If you thin the shot you swung too flat—make sure you follow the slope through the ball. If you catch it fat, you swung too steep. Try taking the club back along the slope in your takeaway without lifting it into the air.

Step 4

Make sure you release the club (let your right hand cross over your left) after impact, and swing as far into your follow-through as possible.

DON'T DO THIS...
From a normal stance, you have to take the club back very steep or you'll crash into your right leg.

143

SHOT

75 Chip From an Uphill Lie

Here are 5 keys to a clean shot when you're leaning away from the hole

KEY MOVE

At impact, think about keeping the shaft leaning forward and your hands and clubhead finishing low. This will prevent you from popping the ball up and leaving it short.

LOW FIVE

• Keep your hands low through impact—don't try to swing them "up the slope."

LEAN RIGHT

• Lean away from the target and keep your weight back. Then treat the shot like a chip from a flat lie.

SHOT RECIPE	
CLUB	One more than standard
AIM	At target
STANCE	Weight favors right foot
BALL POSITION	Between center and left heel
SWING	Standard chip swing
FEEL	Hands finish low

The Situation

You're within easy chipping distance of the green, but the lie dictates that your front foot will be higher than your back foot.

The Solution

For any chip it's important to play the ball where your swing bottoms out. When you add slope to the equation it's difficult to know exactly where that is (one reason why you often hit shots from this lie fat or thin). Here are the setup dos and don'ts when chipping from an upslope:

DON'T...

...lean into the hill. True, you normally set your weight forward on a chip shot, but not in this situation.

...try to scoop the ball. It's a fundamentally unsound move, and the hill will provide you with more than enough "lift." In fact, scooping is what you're trying to guard against.

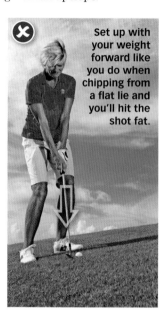

Set up with your weight forward like you do when chipping from a flat lie and you'll hit the shot fat.

DO...

...take one more club than you would playing from a level lie at the same distance; i.e., a sand wedge instead of a lob wedge. The slope adds loft.

...play the ball forward in your stance (between the center and your left heel).

...lean away from the target so that most of your weight is on your right foot. Forward press your hands just ahead of your zipper so the shaft leans toward the target.

DIFFICULTY LEVEL

0	1	2	3	4	5

Get ball position right and this becomes a fairly straightforward play.

1. SET IT

- Play the ball back in your stance and make sure to swing down, just like you would when hitting an iron shot from the fairway.
- If you try to pick the ball cleanly off the ground you'll likely hit it thin.

2. WEIGH IT

- Set the majority of your weight on your left leg at address and keep it there.
- An easy way to make sure that your weight stays on your left side is to keep your chest ahead of the ball (closer to the target) throughout.

3. STRIKE IT

- Make sure the logo on the back of your glove points at the target at impact. This will help you strike the ball with a square clubface.
- Don't baby this shot—make an aggressive chip swing (your clubs can handle it).

DANGER!
If you play high-bounce lob and sand wedges (which don't interact well with hard ground), use your gap or pitching wedge.

SHOT

76
Chip From Hardpan

With these 3 keys, the only thing hard thing about this shot is the ground

145

The Situation
Your ball has come to rest on some hard ground around the green.

The Solution
The biggest key to hitting the ball off any unforgiving surface is to make sure the club hits the ground—don't ever try to pick these shots clean. Hit the ball *then* dig into the dirt. Follow the steps at left to make that happen.

SHOT RECIPE	
CLUB	Gap or pitch wedge
AIM	At target
STANCE	Weight favors left foot
BALL POSITION	Between center and left heel
SWING	Aggressive chip swing
FEEL	Swing down!

DIFFICULTY LEVEL

0	1	2	3	4	5

It's tough to hit soft shots when you make an aggressive swing. If you get this one close, take a bow.

77 How to Chip From the Rough

Get it close from the deep stuff with 6 different grip/ball position combinations

The Situation

Your approach missed the green only by a few yards. Unfortunately, this particular green is guarded on all sides by rough. You can see your ball, but you're not sure your regular chipping motion is going to get it on the green and close enough for you to one-putt.

The Solution

This is the kind of lie that separates great players from merely good ones. Talented golfers know how to adapt trusted moves to unique situations. In this case, you want to use your regular chip swing, but add to it some steepness (to get the ball out) and distinct stance and grip positions (to knock the ball the correct distance).

DIFFICULTY LEVEL

| 0 | 1 | 2 | 3 | 4 | 5 |

It's a simple shot and the adjustments make it easy to get the ball close, but you never really know how your club is going to react in rough.

146

SQUARE FACE
- Set the clubface square to the target. This gives you more area on the face with which to strike the ball.
- You need a broader strike area because you don't know how the club will react in the grass.

BACK OFF!
- Stand farther away from the ball. This sets your hands lower and adds bounce to the club (to help push it through the rough). It also steepens your shoulder turn—a plus from this lie.

SHOT RECIPE

CLUB	Sand wedge
AIM	Standard
STANCE	Farther from ball
BALL POSITION	Back (low) or forward (high)
SWING	At 75% force
FEEL	Club slips under the ball

HOW TO CHIP FROM ROUGH

Step 1

Address the ball like normal and then stand back from it a little (feel like your hands are lower than usual and in a pre-cocked position).

- **For a regular chip,** position the ball in the center of your stance.
- **For a higher chip,** play the ball forward of center.
- **For a lower chip,** play the ball back of center.
- **If you're chipping to a close pin,** choke down on the club and take an open, narrow stance.
- **If you're chipping to a far pin,** widen your stance and stay square to the ball.

KEY MOVE

Step 2

With your adjustments in place, make your regular chipping motion with about 75-percent force (you want to stay extra balanced when chipping from rough). Let your steeper swing get the ball out. Feel like the club is slipping under the ball and popping it up more than it pops it forward.

78 Chip From Deep Rough

Take practice swings until you can cut through the grass

The Situation

Your approach shot landed in thick greenside rough (deeper than the stuff on the opposite page). To save par, you're going to have to dig this ball out and land it close. That's a tall order.

The Solution

The key is to turn your body with your swing. Because the ball is so deep in the grass, you think you have to chop at it with your arms, but that's a sure recipe for inconsistent contact.

Tour players will take 10-15 practice swings from unfamiliar lies like this to get the right feel.

Step 1

With your sand wedge or lob wedge, line up square to the target line in a balanced stance with the ball positioned forward of center.

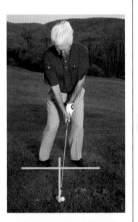

Step 2

Swing back easy so that your hands are at least waist-high when the shaft points into the air.

Step 3

Swing through to a finish that's a mirror image of your backswing: hands at waist height and the shaft pointing straight up. The key is to turn your body through the ball. This will help you add feel to the shot and create a more consistent result.

147

DIFFICULTY LEVEL

0 1 2 3 4 5

A lot of golfers get to this spot in two and then walk off the green with a double. This swing, however, gives you a consistent feel, so you should get the ball within 10 feet every time.

SHOT RECIPE	
CLUB	Sand wedge or lob wedge
AIM	Standard
STANCE	Well-balanced
BALL POSITION	Slightly forward of center
SWING	Waist-high to waist-high
FEEL	Fluid—the club should "glide"

SHOT

79

How to Hit a Flop Shot

You don't need to be perfect to be effective

148

What It Is
A lofted short shot that carries as high in the air as it does over the ground.

When to Use It
When you're within 40 yards of your target with a hazard or a ledge in front that takes away the bump-and-run option, or any situation where you need the ball to fly high and land soft.

How to Hit It
First, stop thinking about this as a "flop shot" and start thinking of this as a high pitch shot. Sounds easier, right? With today's technology and 60-degree and even 62-degree wedges, the days when you needed the perfect timing of a Tour pro are over. Instead, keep your hands quiet and let the club do the work of lofting this ball high.

DIFFICULTY LEVEL

0	1	2	3	4	5

The reason this shot is difficult is because most amateurs don't practice it. Success with the flop shot—or high pitch shot—is driven by feel and experience.

FLOP OPTION
- When you can't run the ball up or the pin is tucked tight on the edge you're hitting toward, the high-lofted pitch is your go-to play.

MAKE IT FAST
- Flop shots are short shots, but make no mistake—these are full-swing plays.
- Try to hit the ball "soft" and it will come up way short of your target.

SHOT RECIPE	
CLUB	Lob wedge
AIM	A shade left of target
STANCE	Slightly open
BALL POSITION	Slightly forward of center
SWING	3/4 backswing to full finish
FEEL	Quiet hands

HOW TO LOFT THE BALL HIGH, SHORT AND SOFT

KEY MOVE

Step 1

Grab your lob wedge or most lofted club. If you don't carry a lob wedge, you're putting yourself at a disadvantage. Check out the loft it generates even from a square setup! (Step on the face of any club and the shaft will tell you how high the ball will launch at impact).

Step 2

Take your address with the clubface slightly open and aimed five yards left of your target. Position the ball just forward of center and weaken your grip until the Vs formed by your forefingers and thumbs point a shade left of your shirt buttons. Lastly, choke down one inch on the handle.

Step 3

Hinge the club up with your wrists in your backswing, but keep the rest of your hands quiet. Adjust the length of your backswing depending on how far you need to fly it, but keep in mind that this is a control shot and never make more than a three-quarter backswing. This shorter swing will help you achieve the easy tempo and transition you want for this shot. A 75-percent backswing with a 60-degree lob wedge rotated slightly open should give you about 50 yards of distance.

Step 4

Swing down with almost full force. The mistake most people make on this shot is leaving it short. The photo at left shows the trajectory of a lob wedge—you can see that this ball will travel a lot higher than the distance it carries over the ground. A more aggressive swing will create an even higher ballflight and more spin so you can land the ball softly near tucked pins from short distance.

Can't Hit a Flop? Try Bending Your Left Wrist

It's the secret to creating loft

When most golfers attempt a high-lofted flop or lob, they either hit the shot fat and short or blade the ball across the green. That happens because the leading edge makes contact with the turf. Good flop artists hit the ground with the bottom of the wedge, just like they do when blasting the ball from a bunker.

Try this the next time you need to hit a lobber. At address, set your feet shoulder-width apart, **position the ball in the center of your stance and set your hands even with your zipper Note how this creates a slight cup in your left wrist.** The secret is to maintain the cup throughout your swing. When you do, the bottom of your wedge will skip off the turf and you'll catch the shot clean. Lose the cup and you'll hit the shot fat or thin.

Maintaining the cup in your left wrist also adds to the loft built into your wedge, enabling you to hit a higher, softer shot with the same swing. As long as you keep the cup, you can make as aggressive a swing as you want. The harder you swing, the higher and softer the shot will fly.

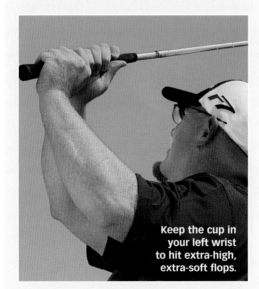

Keep the cup in your left wrist to hit extra-high, extra-soft flops.

149

80 Ball Against the Fringe

If there's grass behind the ball, ditch your putter and putt with the edge of your wedge

GRASS FACTOR
- You could opt for your putter here, but the grass behind the ball may interfere with your stroke or inhibit pure contact, causing the ball to roll off line.

HIT HERE
- With the leading edge of your pitching wedge, strike the ball on its equator. This is one situation where it pays to catch it thin.

SHOT RECIPE

CLUB	Pitching wedge
AIM	At target
STANCE	Standard putting stance
BALL POSITION	Off left heel
SWING	Straight back-and-through
FEEL	Like you're thinning it

The Situation

The ball is sitting where the rough and the fringe meet. The lack of grass under the ball means you have no cushion, while the heavy grass behind the ball makes solid contact nearly impossible.

The Solution

While the term "bladed wedge" may send shivers down your spine, it's the perfect shot for this lie. The shorter length of your wedge gives you more control than if you tried to chip the ball with your hybrid, and its sharper leading edge slides through the heavy grass much easier than your putter.

HOW TO BLADE IT CLOSE

KEY MOVE

Step 1
Use your pitching wedge (it has the straightest edge of all your wedges) and grip it like you would your putter. Address the ball like you're setting up for a putt and align the lead edge with the equator of the ball.

Step 2
Make your normal putting stroke. Your goal is to strike the ball on its equator with the lead edge. Keep your body still—this is an arms-only shot. The ball will bounce first but roll smooth after a few feet.

DIFFICULTY LEVEL

0 1 2 3 4 5

As long as you treat your wedge like a putter and make a level stroke, you'll have no problems getting up-and-down from this lie.

150

SHOT 81 Pop Shot From the Fringe

This finesse shot takes the guesswork out of club and shot selection

What It Is
A soft pop shot that lands a foot or two past the fringe and rolls slowly to the hole.

When to Use It
When you're just off the green but sitting on scraggly fringe that could make the ball bounce off line.

How to Hit It
There's not much to this shot, making it the automatic choice when you're caught up in the fringe. Your main priority is to hit the ball as softly as possible. Problem is, whenever you try to hit the ball soft, you end up decelerating and hit too far behind the ball. To keep this from happening and leaving the ball short of the hole or in the fringe, grip way down on your sand wedge (a good 3 inches). This effectively shortens the club and reduces speed at impact, allowing you to make your normal chipping stroke without worrying about swinging slow or hitting the ball too hard.

KEY MOVE

CHOKE DOWN
- It's an easy adjustment that gives you a softer shot with your regular chip swing.

LIE CHECK
- If your ball is on bumpy fringe or you have less than 15 feet to the hole, use your lob wedge, but keep the same amount of choke.

ROLL OUT
- The pop shot doesn't produce much spin, so plan for the ball to run out twice the amount it travels in the air.

DIFFICULTY LEVEL

0	1	2	3	4	5

This one's a no-brainer, but like most short shots you need practice to develop a feel for distance control and how the club reacts in the fringe.

SHOT RECIPE	
CLUB	Sand wedge
AIM	Left of target
STANCE	Standard chipping stance
BALL POSITION	Just forward of center
SWING	Standard chip motion
FEEL	Regular speed with a choke

On The
Green

Make the Putt–From Anywhere!

Learn to control your stroke to overcome bumps, rises, breaks and severe grain and get the ball to tap-in range at worst

GO TO ANY PRACTICE putting green and you'll see players roll a few balls from 12 feet and call it a day. That's practice, but is it practical? If all you face are straight 12-footers, then yes. But when it comes down to getting the ball into the hole on the course, you need to do it from all distances, against all kinds of breaks and on different types of grass (not to mention during different times of the day). The 12-footer, however, is a start—make it a base from which to adjust to the putt at hand. Then add in the specialty tips on the following pages to fine-tune your aim, stroke length and pace to knock the ball close from just about anywhere on the green. Your primary goal is to always make the putt on your first try. This chapter makes sure you don't need a third or fourth.

82 How to Sink a 100-Foot Putt

Look at the hole during your practice stroke to give yourself a chance

GET THE FEEL

- To dial in the right speed, make your practice strokes while looking at the hole.
- When you hit the putt, try to re-create the feel of your practice stokes.

The Situation

You've left your approach short on a large green and now stand over a 100-foot putt, which you'll need to at least two-putt to save par.

The Problem

You never practice this shot—and even if you wanted to, where would you find a practice green big enough? That means you don't have any reference for how to hit this putt

UPSTRIKE

- If you hit down on the ball the putt will come up way short.
- Play it forward so you catch it on the upswing.

END RESULT

- As your putt slows, the break affects it more, so pay special attention to the last 20 feet of this putt.

154

DIFFICULTY LEVEL

0 1 2 3 4 5

Even Tour pros have difficulty two-putting from here because it's such a difficult shot to practice.

HOW TO GET CLOSE FROM WAY DOWNTOWN

Studies have shown that people who look at the hole while putting make more long putts than players looking at the hole. You might not be comfortable with that, but at least make a point to look at the hole during your practice strokes and then hit your putt. *[For more on this technique, see Shot 89.]*

You don't need to rush your pre-putt time, but don't lollygag either—you want those muscle memories to be fresh when you putt. Place the ball just slightly forward in your stance so you don't hit it on a downward stroke and come up short. Unless Lewis and Clark are in your foursome, you won't be able to read every break of this green, but pay special attention to the last third of this putt because that's where it will break the most.

KEY MOVE

Feel the distance with your eyes
When you focus your eyes on the ball (and not the target) you impede your ability to "feel" the distance to the hole on lag putts. That's why you should make your practice strokes looking at the hole. Think of it as playing a game of "catch" with the cup. As you peer at your target and get a read on speed and distance, make long, smooth pendulum practice strokes. Then, step in and roll the ball with the same feel.

155

Play the ball forward so you hit up on it. If you catch the ball on a downward strike, you'll come up short.

SHOT RECIPE	
CLUB	Putter
AIM	Normal
STANCE	Normal
BALL POSITION	Slightly forward
SWING	Long pendulum
FEEL	Imitate practice strokes

SHOT

83

Uphill Putt

The green rises, but your stroke doesn't. Keep it level to get this putt to the hole.

The Situation
You're on the green but stuck on the low side of a ridge and putting to an uphill hole. Not only do you need to read the slope correctly, but you need to give this putt enough juice to make it up the hill.

The Solution
The first thing you want to do is find out how the slope will affect your putt. Walk to the low side of the hole, about halfway between the ball and the hole. From here you can "triangulate" the putt and see where you need to aim.

SHOT RECIPE	
CLUB	Putter
AIM	Read green from low side
STANCE	Wider than normal
BALL POSITION	Slightly back of center
SWING	Standard
FEEL	Make a level blow

DIFFICULTY LEVEL

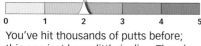

0   1   2   3   4   5

You've hit thousands of putts before; this one just has a little incline. There's nothing especially tricky about it.

156

KEY MOVE

STEP 1
- Once you've found your aiming line, address the ball with a wider stance than normal and the ball slightly back in your stance.
- These adjustments will encourage you to strike the ball with a level stroke in the center of the putterface—a must when putting uphill.

STEP 2
- Make your normal putting stroke.
- While your head stays still on every putt, it's especially important for it to remain stationary here since anything less than solid contact won't get you home.

SHOT 84

Downhill Putt

Forget about the hole. Focus on the "speed spot" to drain this one or leave it close.

The Situation

The good news is you're on the green, but the bad news is you're over the hole, facing a downhill putt on a fairly quick green. In this position, many players focus on the hole and roll the putt way past it, or get too timid and leave the ball way short.

The Solution

Walk to the low side of this putt, halfway between the ball and the hole, and get a sense of the slope. Use your imagination and envision how your putt will behave. Will it break? If so, where? How far do you need to hit it before the slope can carry it the rest of the way?

Next, identify your "speed spot." That's the spot you need to putt to so the slope will carry the ball to the cup. That spot is now your target—keep the hole out of your mind. If you've determined that this putt will break, then move your speed spot to the side to allow for how you think the putt will curve. Try to make a rhythmic, pendulum-like stroke and commit to the spot—if you waffle mentally, you'll leave the putt short.

DIFFICULTY LEVEL

0	1	2	3	4	5

This is a hard putt because you need to interpret the slope correctly and totally commit to your plan. This is tough to do if you haven't experienced a lot of success on a shot.

KEY MOVE

AIM HERE

- Determine the "speed spot" (the point where the putt really picks up speed as it travels downhill) and make it your target.

SHOT RECIPE	
CLUB	Putter
AIM	At the "speed spot"
STANCE	Weight on front foot
BALL POSITION	Center
SWING	Pendulum-like
FEEL	Total commitment

SHOT

85

Putt From a Top Tier

It's only half a putt—the rest is gravity

The Situation
Your approach shot carried farther than you wanted it to. When the ball finally landed, it came to rest on the back tier of a two-tiered green that slopes back to front.

The Solution
Most golfers think of this as a downhill putt, but it's a bit more complicated than that. If you don't get the ball to the precipice, the ball will stay on the tier you're standing on, so you can't hit it soft like you do on a straight downhiller. Your goal is to roll the ball at the slowest possible speed that allows it to just reach the cusp of the tier. The rest is watching gravity do its thing.

How to Putt to a Lower Tier
You use intermediate targets all the time. In this situation, it's the edge of the top tier—make that your final target. In a sense it's easier than a level putt because you only need to roll the ball roughly half the distance to the cup.

DIFFICULTY LEVEL

0 1 2 3 4 5

Even if you roll it perfectly to the edge, there's no way to know for sure how much speed the ball will pick up as it travels the slope. A two-putt in this situation is a cause for celebration.

158

DROP POINT
- Don't think of the hole as your target.
- Aim for a spot on the cusp of the tier you're standing on. Once you have it, commit to it.
- You want the ball to almost stop before it begins rolling down the hill.

ROLL IT PURE
- Other than the tier, this is like any putt—same posture, same alignment, same everything.
- Don't slow down to hit it soft. Simply shorten your stroke (but make sure you keep it even on both sides of the ball).

EYE YOUR TARGET
Make a few practice strokes looking at your intermediate target (the cusp). Eyeballing the distance will help you feel it in your stroke.

Roll the ball at the slowest possible speed to reach the cusp, then let gravity take over.

SHOT RECIPE	
CLUB	Putter
AIM	At intermediate target
STANCE	Standard
BALL POSITION	Standard
SWING	Standard
FEEL	Roll the ball to the cusp

SHOT 86 Putt From a Low Tier

Get the ball all the way up the slope so it doesn't roll back to you

The Situation
You're on a nice, flat section of the green, but wait—the pin is 30 feet away and resting on the next tier up.

The Solution
In this situation, you're dealing with two putts: 1) the one that gets the ball up the hill and, 2) the one that covers the upper tier bewteen the cusp and the hole. Unfortunately, there isn't a magic formula to decipher these two distances and come up with an ideal stroke length, but it isn't a bad idea to add the pace you think will cover the line on the top tier to the force you need to get it all the way up the slope.

HOW TO PUTT TO AN ELEVATED TIER
Set your eyes over ball and your hands under your shoulders, and keep your eyes and sternum still at impact. The more solid your contact, the more likely you'll have enough steam to cover the slope and the overall distance of the putt.

As you make your practice strokes, imagine you're "bowling" the ball up the hill. If you're putting from the left side of the hole (cup off to your right), expect the slope to bend the ball to the right. The opposite is true if you're putting from the right side of the hole.

Add the pace you need to get the ball up the slope to the one needed to roll it from the cusp to the hole.

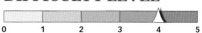

It's a tricky putt, but stay true to your setup and stroke fundamentals.

DIFFICULTY LEVEL

0 1 2 3 4 5

It's easier than putting to a low tier. You have more control of the ball's overall roll, and there's no chance gravity will cause the ball to roll off the green.

SHOT RECIPE	
CLUB	Putter
AIM	At target
STANCE	Standard
BALL POSITION	Standard
SWING	Standard
FEEL	"Bowl" the ball up to the tier

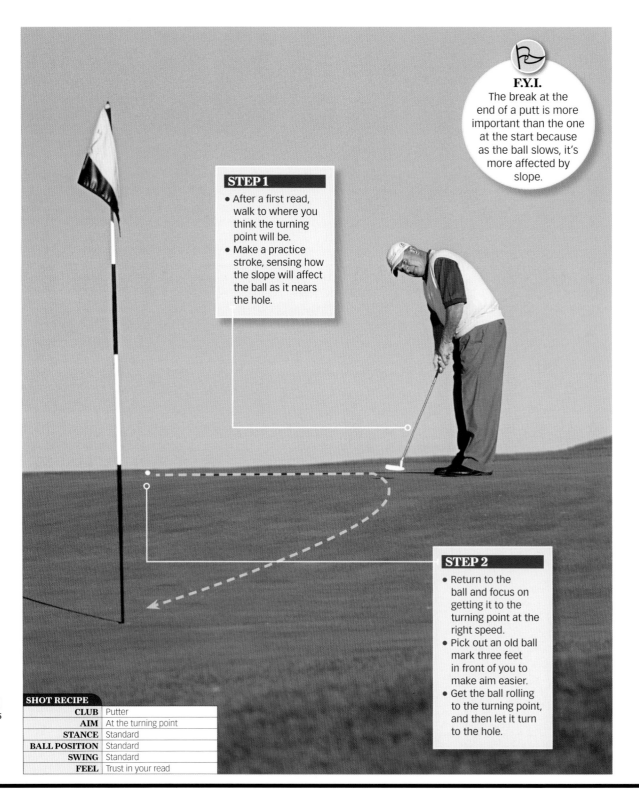

SHOT

87

How to Putt a Double-Breaker

Cut the putt in half to avoid a bad result

160

The Situation

You have a long putt, but that doesn't concern you. What does is the fact that this baby is going to turn left at the start and then bend to the right as it gets closer to the hole. You don't have a clue as to where you should aim, or which break—the one at the start or the one at the finish—will have a greater affect on the roll.

The Solution

Don't get overwhelmed by a long, double-breaking putt. Simplify it by finding the turning point: the spot where the break changes direction. *Follow the steps at right.*

DIFFICULTY LEVEL

0	1	2	3	4	5

Double the break means double the chances that you'll read the putt incorrectly, but this technique will make sure you get home in two.

F.Y.I.
The break at the end of a putt is more important than the one at the start because as the ball slows, it's more affected by slope.

STEP 1
- After a first read, walk to where you think the turning point will be.
- Make a practice stroke, sensing how the slope will affect the ball as it nears the hole.

STEP 2
- Return to the ball and focus on getting it to the turning point at the right speed.
- Pick out an old ball mark three feet in front of you to make aim easier.
- Get the ball rolling to the turning point, and then let it turn to the hole.

SHOT RECIPE	
CLUB	Putter
AIM	At the turning point
STANCE	Standard
BALL POSITION	Standard
SWING	Standard
FEEL	Trust in your read

88 How to Putt on Windy Days

If it's breezy, brace your stance for a purer roll

The Situation

The wind is howling. It's not only affecting shots generated by your full swing, it's messing with your putting, too. You can almost feel the breeze blow your stroke off line. The ball isn't behaving very well, either.

The Solution

Wind is a serious concern when you putt, especially if it's gusting. When you take your normal putting stance with a taller posture and your feet close together, you make it easy for the breeze to jostle you out of position. Make the changes outlined here to brace yourself—and your stroke—against the wind.

KEY MOVE

Set your feet outside your shoulders and choke down on the grip.

Pull your chest closer to the ball by flexing your knees and bending more from your hips.

Position the ball in the center of your stance.

ON WINDY DAYS

- Move your feet outside your shoulders for extra balance and play the ball in the center of your stance.
- Grip down on the shaft and flex your knees so that your chest is closer to the ball.
- **This compact address position is less affected by wind, allowing you to keep your stroke on line.**

ON CALM DAYS

- Take a shoulder-width stance and play the ball just forward of center.
- Stand in a taller posture with just a touch of knee flex.

DIFFICULTY LEVEL

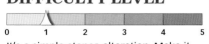

| 0 | 1 | 2 | 3 | 4 | 5 |

It's a simple stance alteration. Make it and drain more putts on windy days.

SHOT RECIPE	
CLUB	Putter
AIM	At target
STANCE	Feet outside shoulders
BALL POSITION	Center
SWING	Standard
FEEL	Like you're "braced"

161

89

How to Lag It Close

Here's two ways to make sure your second putt is an easy one

The Situation

You hit the green with your approach but left it a good 30 feet from the pin. You chances of holing this putt are slim; your chances of 3-putting are good, especially if you don't get the speed right.

The Solution

There are two easy ways to dial in the correct speed so you don't leave your lag putt too far from the hole. The first taps the power of your eyes and their ability to naturally decipher distances and control what you do with your putter without you even having to think about it *[Method 1]*. If that method doesn't work for you, follow the steps at far right to build an inventory of strokes that putt the ball 3 distinct distances *[Method 2]*. One of these strokes will suffice for most lag situations.

IMPORTANT: The secret to lagging putts is to control speed with stroke length, not speeding up or slowing down your motion. Your rhythm and tempo stay the same for every putt; only the length of your stroke changes.

DIFFICULTY LEVEL

| 0 | 1 | 2 | 3 | 4 | 5 |

This one is a no-brainer. With a little practice, you'll start lagging putts like a cagey Tour pro.

162

EYE THE PRIZE
- Look at the hole while making practice strokes.
- Your eyes tell your body how long a backstroke is needed to get the ball to tap-in range.

METHOD 2: BUILD A STROKE-DISTANCE INVENTORY

Before your round, go to the practice putting green and find a flat spot on the green (you don't need a hole). Settle into your stance and putt the ball. Then...

Step 1
Take the putterhead back to your right toe using your normal tempo and rhythm. Once the ball stops rolling, walk of the distance (it'll be about 18 to 20 feet).

Step 2
Settle into your stance and make another stroke. This time, take your hands back to your right toe (giving you about 28-30 feet of distance).

Step 3
Make a third stroke. On this one, take your hands outside your right toe. When you walk this one off you'll find this backstroke length gives you 38 to 40 feet of distance.

163

METHOD 1: GAUGE STROKE LENGTH WITH YOUR EYES

- Take your stance then turn your head to the hole and make practice strokes while looking at the cup. Make three concentrated practice strokes. As you make each one, your eyes send signals to your arms and hands, directing them to take your putter back the correct length to match the distance they've calculated.
- When you complete your third backstroke, hold your position and look back to see how far back your eyes told you to take the putterhead. When you go to stroke the putt for real, take the putter back to that same spot. Use your normal speed, rhythm and tempo—the ball will end up close.

SHOT RECIPE	
CLUB	Putter
AIM	At target
STANCE	Standard
BALL POSITION	Standard
SWING	Practice while looking at hole
FEEL	Change length, not speed

KEY MOVE

Hands outside toe.

Hands to toe.

Putter to toe.

With this drill you'll learn to putt the ball three distinct distances in about five minutes (just match the distance to the backstroke length). It's the same principle as knowing how far you hit each iron in your bag. When you're caught at distances between the ones in your inventory, fine-tune your stroke by either taking the putter back a little farther or a little shorter. Your goal from long range is to two-putt, and this method makes it very easy.

90
Short Breaking Putt

Try different perspectives to find the right line

The Situation

You've left yourself a 6-footer and need it to save par or post your best score ever. You're steamed because it's clear that the ball is going to curve hard on its path to the hole.

The Solution

Ever wonder what Tour pros are talking about when they say "I saw the lines very clearly today?" What they mean is that they actually see the ball roll on its route to the cup. This kind of visualization is one of the most important parts of green reading, and you can improve your ability to do it by changing the position from where you read your putts. The following 3-step procedure. It allows you to draw the correct line just like the pros do and make simple work of those tough, short, breaking putts.

164

DIFFICULTY LEVEL

0	1	2	3	4	5

The green-reading steps outlined here are easy to perform, but your ability to decode what you see will come only with experience.

HOW TO DRAIN A BREAKER

Step 1
Start by looking down the "ball-to-hole" line *[yellow dashed]*. If your imagined roll of the putt *[white line]* looks like it will miss to the right if it followed this line…

Step 2
…move over to your right. Find the point where, now, a line drawn from you through the ball will start the ball too far out to the left. Then…

Step 3
… Move back in between these two borders and look for the place that allows you to imagine the putt rolling directly away from you and into the hole. *[Reverse the steps if the ball looks like it will miss to the left in Step 1.]*

TILT TO SEE THE LINE
Once you've found a line that you think will get the ball in the hole, lean your upper body to the right and then to the left. Doing this allows you to confirm the line from both sides of the ball's roll. It's an extra bit of fine-tuning that will make your final read and starting line more exact.

EYE LINES
- If you struggle with green reading, look at the line from as many different angles behind the ball as possible.
- Often, the best line will come to you after seeing a few that obviously won't work.

KEY MOVE

START POINT
- Visualize your putts from the line where they begin—not where they end.
- You have more control of what happens at the start of the putt than you do at the finish.

MIND READER
- Picture the ball rolling along the break you've calculated in your mind's eye before pulling the trigger.

SHOT RECIPE	
CLUB	Putter
AIM	Variable
STANCE	Standard
BALL POSITION	Standard
SWING	Standard
FEEL	Picture the roll—then do it

165

CHAPTER

8

Trick Shots That Work

How to pull off the impossible—
and impress your friends—from
the most difficult and most
unusual lies

AFTER MOST ROUNDS you can wear the clothes you played in to the office the next day. Golf is rarely a dirty affair, but from time to time it will force you to roll up your sleeves and go to work in the trenches, especially when your accuracy really starts to falter. Enter the trick shot—a high-risk, high-reward play that's the swing equivalent of pulling a rabbit out of your hat. The ones you'll learn in this chapter, however, are hardly illusions. They're proven methods that can bring you back from the brink to a par save or better. Moreover, they're fun to practice after you have given your full swing its due on the range. So bring on the water, concrete or a 200-year-old sequoia—this branch of shotmaking allows you to clean up from anywhere.

SHOT 91

Bank-Shot Chip

Save par when you don't have enough green to land even a flop shot

What It Is

A hard chip shot hit into the bank of a hill. The ball shoots straight up after it strikes the hill and lands like a butterfly with sore feet on the green.

When to Use It

You've missed a crowned green to the left or right and settled into a collection area. There's a slope in front of you and, worse yet, very little green between the fringe and the pin. There's not even enough green to hold a high-lofted shot.

How to Hit It

The most important weapon in your short game is your imagination, and you need to use it here. Instead of attempting an impossible flop or skating a chip across the green, bump the ball into the slope in front of you. *Follow the steps at right.*

DIFFICULTY LEVEL

0	1	2	3	4	5

Basically, you have zero room for error. Miss your spot on the slope just 3 feet too high and you're skidding over the green; miss 6 feet low and you won't make it there.

168

FORM A LINE
- Restrict your follow-through and keep the club in line with your hands.

FEET TOGETHER
- Play this shot with your feet close together and your weight leaning slightly to the left.

HOW TO BANK THE BALL CLOSE

Step 1

Find your target on the bank. Generally, it will be a spot about three-quarters up the bank. (Make sure the bank is steep enough so that the force of the ball will cause it to bounce up and not skip forward.)

Step 2

Set up to the ball like you would for a chip shot with your feet close together, your hands pressed forward and your weight favoring the left. The ball should be just a shade back of center in your stance since the last thing you want to do here is hit up on the ball (you'll add loft and miss the bank completely).

169

Step 3

Make an extremely aggressive chip shot without any release and with a limited follow-through [photo, left]. Notice how the hands are still in line with the club and how the club hasn't released.

KEY MOVE

Step on the face of your club to see if it has the loft you need to hit the right spot on the hill.

WHICH CLUB

Here's an easy way to figure out the trajectory of your chips. Take a club and lay it face up along the ground. Now step down on the clubhead so that the shaft rises off the ground. That angle is the trajectory of your chips with that club. Your PW, 9- and 8-iron will give you a high trajectory; use your 5-, 6- and 7-irons when you want to bring the ball in lower.

DANGER!
Miss the hill and you may never see your ball again. Err on using too little loft than too much loft when playing this shot.

...watch it pop up to here...

...and end up next to the hole.

Hit it here...

SHOT RECIPE	
CLUB	Iron
AIM	At target
STANCE	Feet inside shoulders
BALL POSITION	One half-ball back of center
SWING	At 70% speed
FEEL	Hard chip shot

SHOT 92

Driver Off the Deck

From the right lie, this cannon blast brings any par-5 green into range

170

What It Is

A shot hit from the fairway—or just off it—with the most unlikeliest of clubs: your driver.

When to Use It

Your tee shot on a par 5 has landed in the first cut of rough and a little short of your normal full distance. You're beyond the limit of your 3-wood, but you're desperate to get on in two. If the ball is sitting up on the grass, you're in a good position to hit driver again and reach your goal.

How to Hit It

Think of this shot as a power cut you have to catch absolutely pure. Hit it just the tiniest bit fat or thin and your chance at birdie goes right out the window. *Follow the steps at right.*

DIFFICULTY LEVEL

| 0 | 1 | 2 | 3 | 4 | 5 |

In addition to needing turbocharged swing speed, you also need perfect touch to just brush the grass with your club.

SHOT RECIPE	
CLUB	Driver
AIM	Slightly left (open clubface)
STANCE	Just like your 3-wood
BALL POSITION	Between center and left heel
SWING	Full with a shallow approach
FEEL	Like you're brushing the grass

HOW TO DRIVE IT OFF THE DECK

CUT IT ON

- Aim left and open the clubface a few degrees. This gives your 10-degree driver the loft of a 3-wood, but the ball will go farther because of the longer shaft length.

SPEED DEMON

- Other than a good lie, the primary key to hitting this shot is swing speed.
- If you can drive the ball farther than 270 yards and generate more than 105 mph of speed, you can play this shot. If not, use your 3-wood or hit a safe lay-up.

LIE CHECK

- You need the right lie to execute this shot.
- With today's deep-faced drivers, you can't get this shot up in the air from a tight fairway lie (you'll hit it extremely thin).
- The best scenario is a nice lie in the first cut of the rough, where the ball sits on the grass like it's on a tee.

Step 1

Assess the lie. If the ball is sitting up and you can get it in the air, go for it.

The perfect driver-off-the-deck lie.

Step 2

Set up as you would with a 3-wood off the fairway, with the ball positioned halfway between the center of your stance and your left heel [photo, right]. **Make sure you don't lean your hands forward since that takes away loft and you'll need all you can get.** Open the clubface and aim slightly left. This will help you get the ball into the air.

DANGER!
If the heel digs at impact, the face will close quickly, making this a very easy shot to hook. Do your best to just brush the grass.

KEY MOVE

Step 3

It's critical you come into the ball on a shallow angle of attack. Don't take a divot—just brush the grass under the ball. This is a good shot to use into the wind because it's easy to keep low and it will run forever once it hits the ground.

Don't Do This

The worst possible mistake you can make with this swing is approaching the ball on a steep plane or swinging from outside the target line to the inside. You'll take too much turf and de-loft the clubface, giving you almost zero chance of getting the ball in the air.

171

SHOTS 93 & 94

Mega-Hook/ Mega-Slice

Hey big bender! Pull out these sweeping curves when you can't fly over or under obstacles.

The Situation

You've hooked or sliced the ball off the tee and now your approach to the green is blocked by a tree. The tree is too high to hit over *[Shot 51]* and its branches hang too close to the ground for you to play a low punch *[Shot 50]*. The last thing on your mind is chipping back to safety—you want to advance the ball far down the fairway so you're left with an easy wedge to the green.

The Solution

Remember that hook or slice that got you in this mess? You're going to hit that shot again, but this time on purpose and with an exaggerated setup that will curve the ball one yard for every two yards it flies in the air. Do it correctly and you can expect to generate at least 40 yards of curve with a mid-iron.

DIFFICULTY LEVEL

0	1	2	3	4	5

These shots are based entirely on your setup. Nail your address and you'll pull off these shots with ease. The only trouble is your lie—you're off the fairway and you'll likely be in some tough rough.

SECRET SETUP

- To mega-hook the ball, close the face 45 degrees and pull your right foot back.
- To mega-slice the ball, open the face 45 degrees and pull your left foot back.

172

Big, roping hooks and slices start at your setup— don't do anything different in your swing.

CURVE CONTROL

- Make sure to aim clear of the obstacle.
- Severely opening or closing the clubface will give you 40 yards of curve and 100 yards of carry with a mid-iron.

SHOT RECIPE	
CLUB	Mid-iron
AIM	Way right (hook) or left (slice)
STANCE	Right (hook) or left (slice)
BALL POSITION	Center (hook), left toe (slice)
SWING	Full back to full finish
FEEL	Normal, everyday motion

HOW TO HIT A MEGA-HOOK

Step 1

Grab a mid-iron, hold it out in front of you and shut down the face a good 45 degrees.

Step 2

Take your stance, position the ball in the center, and aim way right of your final target (or just to the right of the right-side edge of the tree). Sole your club on the ground (keep that clubface closed) and pull your right foot back.

This setup is designed to give you about 40 yards of hook. You don't have to make any changes to your swing other than rolling your forearms a bit faster through impact. The shot will fly low, travel about 100 yards and curve like crazy.

HOW TO HIT A MEGA-SLICE

Step 1

Grab a mid-iron, hold it out in front of you and open the face a good 45 degrees.

Step 2

Take your stance, position the ball off your left toe, and aim way left of your final target (or just to the left of the left-side edge of the tree). Sole your club on the ground (keep that clubface open) and pull your left foot back.

This setup is designed to give you about 40 yards of slice. Don't make any changes to your motion. Swing like you would from a nice lie in the fairway and the curve you're looking for will take shape automatically.

173

SHOT

95

Left-Handed Punch-Out

Can't take your stance? Take a swing from the other side.

What It Is

A little punch swing you hit with the club turned upside-down and from a left-handed stance with a left-handed grip.

When to Use It

When your ball comes to rest against the base of a tree, a bush or even an O.B. marker—anything that prohibits you from taking your normal stance and knocking the ball forward.

How to Hit It

"Hit" is the wrong word—after gripping the club like a lefty, you're going to "putt" the ball back into play. You could take a penalty and a drop, but that still might leave you with a nasty lie. A left-handed punch at least gets you back in the fairway where you can attack the pin with your next shot.

DIFFICULTY LEVEL

| 0 | 1 | 2 | 3 | 4 | 5 |

You probably don't swing your clubs left-handed very often, inviting the chance for a whiff on this shot. Hit this one well and they'll toast you in the grill room.

WRIST LOCK
- The last thing you want to do with this shot is hit it with a lot of wrist action. That adds extra arc to your shot, increasing your chances of bottoming out too early or late.
- Lock your wrists and make a smooth, left-handed putting stroke using your shoulders.

FLIP IT
- Rotate the club so that it points at your target with the toe section hanging down.
- Set the toe (the fattest portion of the clubhead) directly behind the ball—that's your strike area.

Not ideal, but not unplayable. A lefty stance and a smooth putting stroke is all you need to get back on the short stuff.

LEFT-HAND LOW
- Grip your sand wedge left-hand low, with your right hand at the top of the handle.

Make a few practice swings so you won't jab at it.

SHOT 96 Back-Handed Slap Save

Show the green your backside and advance the ball with ease

What It Is
An abrupt punch you hit with your back facing the target.

When to Use It
Any time you can't take your normal right-handed stance. You could opt to hit this left-handed *[see Shot 95, opposite page]*, but this one will give you a little more pop (expect a good 20 yards from a decent strike) and is easier to execute because you get to use your dominant hand.

How to Hit It
Ever do triceps pull-down exercises in the gym? That motion is very similar to the one you need here. *Follow the steps at right.*

HOW TO MAKE A LEFT-HANDED SAVE

Step 1
After flipping your sand wedge upside-down (toe pointing to the ground) and gripping the club left-handed, take your stance with the ball positioned off your left foot. This will increase your chances of solid contact.

Step 2
Since you're only looking to advance the ball a few yards (bad things happen when you try to hit this shot too hard), swing the club like it's your putter—think of it as a big left-handed putt.

KEY MOVE
Before you hit this shot, make a few practice swings from a similar lie nearby. Find a leaf and stroke it like it's the ball, taking extra care to make contact using the fat part of the toe section on your club.

Step 1
Choose one of your wedges (these have the largest faces and you'll benefit from a broader hitting area since you won't be looking at the ball during contact).

Step 2
Turn your back to the target, stand about a half-foot to the left side of the ball and grip your wedge with your right hand only in the middle of the handle. Flip your club around so that it faces the target and rests on its toe.

Step 3
Cock your club up by bending your right elbow (keep your upper arm as still as possible). Add just a touch of wrist hinge.

Step 4
Straighten your arm and slap the clubhead into the back of the ball. Make sure you accelerate all the way to the ball so that the club doesn't flip past your hands.

175

DIFFICULTY LEVEL

| 0 | 1 | 2 | 3 | 4 | 5 |

This is a trick shot that's actually very easy to pull off with a little practice. The only danger is catching it thin. Even then it's enough to get you back into play.

SHOT RECIPE	
CLUB	Sand wedge
AIM	Toward safety
STANCE	Left-handed
BALL POSITION	Off left foot
SWING	Putting stroke
FEEL	Smooth stroke to advance it

SHOT RECIPE	
CLUB	Any wedge
AIM	Toward safety
STANCE	Back facing target
BALL POSITION	To the side of right foot
SWING	Up-and-down slap
FEEL	Like a triceps pull-down

SHOT 97

Blast With One Foot Out of the Bunker

176

You can't take a regular stance. Big deal. Step back on the slope and swing down the hill.

The Situation

Your approach shot landed in the back edge of a greenside bunker. When you set up to the ball, you have to place your feet so close together that the ball position moves back to your right foot. You feel there's no way you can make a proper bunker swing with the ball played so far back.

The Solution

Move your right foot up and out of the sand and place it on the hill behind the bunker. You might think this stance is just as limiting as the one with your feet close together, but it actually turns this tough lie into a regular downhill bunker blast. For that shot, the key is to adjust your body so that your swing is level with the slope.

DIFFICULTY LEVEL

0	1	2	3	4	5

Many players fear the downslope lie even when they can get both feet in the bunker. Add the awkward stance and you've got a very tough shot.

CLOSE IT UP
- Move your right foot back (away from your target line) to close your stance and even your hips.
- If you don't close your stance your right side will be too high.

KEY MOVE

A NEW STANCE
- You might think placing your right foot out of the bunker is weird, but it turns this tricky lie into a regular downhill bunker blast.
- If you match your shoulders and hips to the slope, the ball will pop out like it does from a level lie.

If you set up to this lie with both feet in the sand, the ball will be too far back in your stance for you to slide your club underneath it.

SHOULDER TILT

• Angle your shoulders to the slope and move the ball forward in your stance.
• This will create the more outside-in swing you need to swing down the hill.

HOW TO BLAST OFF ONE FOOT

Step 1

Step your left foot in the sand and move your right foot far enough back on the hill behind the bunker that your hips are level to the slope. Angle your shoulders to the slope and move the ball forward in your stance to promote a more outside-in swing.

Step 2

Once you feel balanced, make your normal bunker motion and focus on swinging down the slope with your left knuckles. Because you've adjusted your body to the slope, the ball should pop out like a regular bunker shot.

Set your right foot on the hill and pull it back to angle your shoulders and hips to the hill.

DANGER!
Make a few practice swings (without touching the sand) to make sure you clear the lip of the hill as you swing back.

SHOT RECIPE	
CLUB	Lob or sand wedge
AIM	At target
STANCE	Closed to target
BALL POSITION	Forward of center
SWING	Hip-high to hip-high
FEEL	Swing down the slope

98 Punch Shot From a Fairway Bunker

Sometimes it's easier to roll your ball to the green than fly it there

178

NO FINISH

- Since all you're looking to do is punch the ball forward out of the bunker, your finish is of little consequence.

F.Y.I.
With a 6-iron, a bunker punch will give you 100 yards of carry and 50 yards of roll. Drop to a 7- or 8-iron to hit a shorter shot.

CLEAR PATH

- The ball will roll most of the way to the green, so try this shot only if there are no obstacles between you and the putting surface.

COPY SETUP

- At impact, you want your hands and clubshaft in the same positions they held at address.

SHOT RECIPE	
CLUB	6-, 7- or 8-iron
AIM	At target
STANCE	Narrow, weight on left side
BALL POSITION	Back of center
SWING	Half back to half through
FEEL	Firm wrists at impact

The Situation

You're in a fairway bunker, but close enough to the green that a full-swing with a short iron would come out too hot and roll off the green.

The Solution

If the front of the green is clear of obstacles, play a punch shot that lands short of the green and works it way on.

HOW TO PUNCH IT ON FROM SAND

Step 1

Choose a 6-, 7- or 8-iron, depending on your distance to the pin *[see the F.Y.I. above left]*. This ball will fly low and run out onto the green. Expect the ball to roll half the distance it carries.

Step 2

Set up with the ball back of center and the shaft leaning forward. Line the clubface square to the target. Take a narrow stance with more of your weight on your left foot and your sternum in front of the ball to create a downward angle of attack *[photo, right]*.

Step 3

Start your swing by hinging your wrists quickly back in a narrow arc. Cut your backswing when your hands reach hip height—that's all the power you'll need.

Step 4

From the top, pinch your knees downward and focus on making ball-first, sand-second contact. Keep your wrists firm at impact— you don't want to break down and lose the clubshaft angle you created at address. The ball will come out hot, so leave lots of room for it to run.

DIFFICULTY LEVEL

0   1   2   3   4   5

This really isn't much different than a punch shot off turf, and most players have a punch shot in their games.

Get your chest in front of the ball and lean the shaft toward the target.

179

Hinge your wrists going back, but keep them firm going down.

SHOT

99

Chip Out of a Bunker

Make a safer—and easier—play on long bunker shots

180

SHALLOW LIE
- If the bunker you're in isn't very steep and your lie is good, bust the ball out using your basic chipping stroke.

NEW DIVOT
- On normal sand shots you want to hit behind the ball.
- When you chip it out of the sand, you want your divot to be on the target side of the ball.

SHOT RECIPE	
CLUB	9-, 8- or 7-iron
AIM	At target
STANCE	Feet close together
BALL POSITION	Center
SWING	Chipping motion
FEEL	Hit the ball then the sand

The Situation

You're stuck in a greenside bunker, about 50 feet from the hole. This is a tough shot even for Tour players.

The Solution

Instead of hitting a long bunker blast (one of the toughest shots you can try), chip the ball out of the bunker. A chip is easier to control once it hits the green and allows you to manage your mis-hits. Even if you leave it short, you'll guarantee bogey. Plus, you don't have to worry about making a big swing and taking the right amount of sand.

HOW TO CHIP IT FROM A BUNKER

Step 1
Take a short iron (7-, 8- or 9-iron, depending on distance) and choke down midway on the grip.

Step 2
Set up with your feet close together and your body leaning forward. Keep everything square to your intended line. Your sternum should be a little in front of the ball and your hands should be pressed forward, making a triangle.

Step 3
Use your regular chipping technique and make a crisp pop on the ball. Try to catch the ball a little before the sand. You'll need more swing speed than your normal chip because the ground breaks away beneath the ball in a bunker and you need to roll it 40-50 feet.

KEY MOVE

Stay firm with your left side. Don't break down and try to scoop the ball.

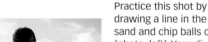

How to Practice It
Practice this shot by drawing a line in the sand and chip balls off it [photo, left]. Your divot should show the club entering the sand at the back of the line and taking a divot in front of the line [photo, right]. This is not an explosion shot, but you should comb the sand enough to take a bit of it out the bunker.

DIFFICULTY LEVEL

Target →

| 0 | 1 | 2 | 3 | 4 | 5 |

The only challenge is selecting the right club for the distance you're facing and making sure you take only *some* sand.

SHOT

100 Splash Shot From the Water

You're going to get wet—a small price for a stroke saved

SAND COPY
Play the splash shot like a sand shot but with the ball positioned in the middle of your stance.

KEY MOVE

SPLASH DOWN
Make a steep and full swing. Your club needs to enter the drink on the most vertical plane possible.

The Situation
The ball is sitting just below the surface of a water hazard, in a spot that makes you think, "I can get that on the green."

The Solution
If you don't mind getting wet, you can pull off this shot. The key is to play the shot like a sand shot. Instead of flying out on a cushion of sand, however, the ball will be forced out on a wave of water.

How to Hit a Splash Shot
To start, pick your target line, then place your right foot in the hazard so the ball is in the middle of your stance. Now bring your left foot down so your stance is slightly open to your target.

Use a pitching wedge (to avoid "bouncing" the club off the water), then make a sharp up-and-down swing. Try to enter the water an inch or two behind the ball and make sure to follow through.

You may not get the ball as close to the hole as you'd like, but the goal all along was to save a shot without having to take a drop.

181

DON'T QUIT
The water will cause your swing to come to a screaming halt, but try to keep your club moving through impact.

SHOT RECIPE	
CLUB	Pitching wedge
AIM	Slightly left of target
STANCE	Slightly open
BALL POSITION	Center
SWING	Extremely steep
FEEL	Don't stop at impact

DIVE IN HERE
Enter the water an inch or two behind the ball, just like you do in a bunker.

DIFFICULTY LEVEL

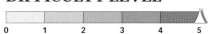

0   1   2   3   4   5

Walking on water might be easier than rescuing your ball from the depths, but it's been done before, and if you pull it off you'll have an amazing story to tell.

SHOT

101
High Chip Off Hardpan

Loft and hardpan go together like fire and ice. Here's how to defy the odds and get the ball close.

The Situation
Your ball is sitting on some hard dirt near the green and a huge deep-faced bunker is between you and the flag. How in the world do you make sure your next shot is a putt?

The Solution
You won't face many short shots tougher than this. You need a high-lofted lob, but since there isn't any grass, you can't slide your clubhead under the ball and pop it into the air. Instead, you need to dig in at the right spot and let the loft of your wedge do all the work.

HIGH DRIFTER
- A low shot won't hold the green; this shot needs loft to carry the bunker and stay on the putting surface once it hits.

FLUFF ENVY
- You could play a normal lob shot if the ball sat here.
- Since you're on the dirt, there's no room to slide your clubhead underneath the ball.

START HERE
- Open your clubface and play the ball an inch back of center.

DANGER!
Hit the ground too far behind the ball and you may never find it again. Err on the side of coming in too steep rather than too flat.

DIFFICULTY LEVEL

| 0 | 1 | 2 | 3 | 4 | 5 |

Make one false move and you'll hit this shot thinner than a bikini model on a crash diet.

182

HOW TO GET IT UP FROM THE DIRT

Step 1

Setup
Use your most lofted wedge. Play the ball an inch back of center and **move your hands forward to create a descending blow**. The butt end of the shaft should point to your left hip. That helps you cheat your weight to your left side. Now make a slight adjustment by opening the clubface to expose the heel of the club, which is less prone to digging in the turf.

Shaft points at left hip.

Step 2

Backswing
Swing your arms straight up without turning your shoulders. This will keep the clubface open and put you on track for a steep downswing. If you swing too shallow, the clubhead will bounce off the ground and you'll blade the ball. **Take the club almost all the way back** because you need to generate enough clubhead speed to hit the ball twice as far as you would on a normal 15-yard pitch.

Swing your arms almost straight up.

Dig in and move the dirt and and the ball to the target.

Step 3

Contact
Drive the heel of your club aggressively into the dirt behind the ball. By leading with the heel [inset photo], you expose the bounce of the club and add loft to your shot. The club isn't going to dig much, so you have a little margin for error behind the ball. **Think about moving the dirt with the ball** and make sure to rotate your hips and chest left of the target. This will keep the face open and prevent the toe from entering the turf.

The secret to this shot is digging the heel into the dirt.

SHOT RECIPE	
CLUB	Lob wedge
AIM	Slightly left of target
STANCE	Slightly open
BALL POSITION	One inch back of center
SWING	Aggressive chop
FEEL	Dig the heel into the dirt

183

THE TOP 100 TEACHERS IN AMERICA

A quick look at the nation's most exclusive—and talented—team of teaching experts

MIKE ADAMS
Facility: Hamilton Farms G.C., Gladstone, N.J.
Website: www.mikeadamsgolf.com
Teaching since: 1977
Top 100 since: 1996
See Mike's tips on pages 146, 176

ROB AKINS
Facility: Ridgeway C.C., Germantown, Tenn.
Website: www.robakinsgolf.com
Teaching since: 1987
Top 100 since: 2001

ERIC ALPENFELS
Facility: The Pinehurst G.A., Pinehurst, N.C.
Website: www.pinehurst.com
Teaching since: 1984
Top 100 since: 2001
See Eric's tip on page 31

TODD ANDERSON
Facility: Sea Island Golf Learning Center, St. Simons Island, Ga.
Website: www.seaisland.com
Teaching since: 1984
Top 100 since: 2003

ROBERT BAKER
Facility: Logical Golf, Miami Beach, Fla.
Website: www.logicalgolf.com
Teaching since: 1989
Top 100 since: 1999
See Robert's tip on page 137

RICK BARRY
Facility: Sea Pines Resort, Hilton Head Island, S.C.
Website: www.seapines.com
Teaching since: 1976
Top 100 since: 2005

MIKE BENDER
Facility: Mike Bender Golf Academy at Timacuan C.C., Lake Mary, Fla.
Website: www.mikebender.com
Teaching since: 1990
Top 100 since: 1996

STEVE BOSDOSH
Facility: Members Club at Four Streams, Beallsville, Md.
Website: www.fourstreams.com
Teaching since: 1983
Top 100 since: 2001
See Steve's tips on pages 22, 42, 58, 82, 118, 174

MICHAEL BREED
Facility: Sunningdale C.C., Scarsdale, N.Y.
Website: www.michaelbreed.com
Teaching since: 1986
Top 100 since: 2003
See Mike's tips on pages 90, 98

BRAD BREWER
Facility: Brad Brewer Golf Academy at Shingle Creek Resort, Orlando, Fla.
Website: www.bradbrewer.com
Teaching since: 1984
Top 100 since: 2007

HENRY BRUNTON
Facility: Henry Brunton Golf, Maple, Ontario
Website: www.henrybrunton.com
Teaching since: 1985
Top 100 since: 2005

ANNE CAIN
Facility: Anne Cain Golf Academy, Amelia Island, Fla.
Website: www.annecaingolf.com
Teaching since: 1995
Top 100 since: 2007
See Anne's tips on pages 36, 92, 154

JASON CARBONE
Facility: Jim McLean G.S., Litchfield Park, Ariz.
Website: www.jimmclean.com/usa/wigwam
Teaching since: 1993
Top 100 since: 2007
See Jason's tips on pages 68, 69, 76, 77, 88, 100

DONALD CRAWLEY
Facility: The Boulders Golf Academy, Carefree, Ariz.
Website: www.golfsimplified.com
Teaching since: 1974
Top 100 since: 1999
See Donald's tips on pages 40, 44, 46, 52, 84, 158, 159

JOHN DAHL
Facility: Oxbow C.C., Oxbow, N.D.
Website: www.oxbowcc.com
Teaching since: 1974
Top 100 since: 2003

BILL DAVIS
Facility: Jupiter Hills Club, Tequesta, Fla.
Website: www.jupiterhillsclub.org
Teaching since: 1973
Top 100 since: 1996
See Bill's tip on page 87

MIKE DAVIS
Facility: Walters Golf Academy, Las Vegas, Nev.
Website: www.waltersgolf.com
Teaching since: 1970
Top 100 since: 2007
See Mike's tip on page 175

GLENN DECK
Facility: Pelican Hill Golf Academy, Newport Coast, Calif.
Website: www.pelicanhill.com
Teaching since: 1983
Top 100 since: 2003

DOM DIJULIA
Facility: Dom DiJulia School of Golf, New Hope, Pa.
Website: www.dijuliagolf.com
Teaching since: 1990
Top 100 since: 2007
See Dom's tips on pages 48, 49, 74, 110, 124, 164

JOHN ELLIOT, JR.
Facility: Golden Ocala Golf & Equestrian Club, Ocala, Fla.
Website: www.goldenocala.com
Teaching since: 1970
Top 100 since: 1996

BILL FORREST
Facility: Troon Country Club, Scottsdale, Ariz.
Website: www.trooncc.com
Teaching since: 1978
Top 100 since: 2007
See Bill's tips on pages 41, 140

EDEN FOSTER
Facility: Maidstone Club, East Hampton, N.Y.
Website: www.maidstoneclub.com
Teaching since: 1988
Top 100 since: 2003
See Eden's tips on pages 82, 96, 106, 182

JANE FROST
Facility: Jane Frost Golf School at Sandwich Hollows G.C., Sandwich, Mass.
Website: www.janefrostgolfschools.com
Teaching since: 1982
Top 100 since: 1996

BRYAN GATHRIGHT
Facility: Oak Hills C.C., San Antonio, Tex.
Website: www.oakhillscc.com
Teaching since: 1987
Top 100 since: 2001
See Bryan's tip on page 116, 123

DAVID GLENZ

Facility: David Glenz Golf Academy, Franklin, N.J.
Website: www.davidglenz.com
Teaching since: 1978
Top 100 since: 1996
See David's tips on pages 29, 50, 104, 126, 147, 157

PATRICK GOSS

Facility: Northwestern University, Evanston, Ill.
Website: www.northwestern.edu/athletics
Teaching since: 1993
Top 100 since: 2007

RICK GRAYSON

Facility: Connie Morris Golf Learning Center, Springfield, Mo.
Website: www.rickgraysongolf.com
Teaching since: 1976
Top 100 since: 1996

FRED GRIFFIN

Facility: Grand Cypress Academy of Golf, Orlando, Fla.
Website: www.grandcypress.com
Teaching since: 1980
Top 100 since: 1996

RON GRING

Facility: Gring Golf, Daphne, Ala.
Website: www.gringgolf.com
Teaching since: 1977
Top 100 since: 2003

ROGER GUNN

Facility: Tierra Rejada G.C., Moorpark, Calif.
Website: www.golflevels.com
Teaching since: 1993
Top 100 since: 2007
See Roger's tips on pages 30, 72, 86

MARTIN HALL

Facility: Ibis Golf & C.C., West Palm Beach, Fla.
Website: www.ibisgolf.com
Teaching since: 1978
Top 100 since: 1996

BRUCE HAMILTON

Facility: Spanish Hills C.C., Camarillo, Calif.
Website: www.spanishhills.com
Teaching since: 1973
Top 100 since: 1996

HANK HANEY

Facility: Hank Haney Golf Ranch, McKinney, Tex.
Website: www.hankhaney.com
Teaching since: 1977
Top 100 since: 1996

JIM HARDY

Facility: Jacobsen/Hardy Golf, Houston, Tex.
Website: www.jimhardygolf.com
Teaching since: 1966
Top 100 since: 1996

BUTCH HARMON, JR.

Facility: Butch Harmon School of Golf, Henderson, Nev..
Website: www.butchharmon.com
Teaching since: 1965
Top 100 since: 1996

CRAIG HARMON

Facility: Oak Hill C.C., Rochester, N.Y.
Website: www.oakhillcc.com
Teaching since: 1968
Top 100 since: 1996

SHAWN HUMPHRIES

Facility: Cowboys G.C., Grapevine, Tex.
Website: www.shawnhumphries.com
Teaching since: 1988
Top 100 since: 2005
See Shawn's tips on pages 94, 168, 180

DON HURTER

Facility: Castle Pines G.C., Castle Rock, Colo.
Website: None
Teaching since: 1987
Top 100 since: 2003

ED IBARGUEN

Facility: Duke University G.C., Durham, N.C.
Website: www.golf.duke.edu
Teaching since: 1979
Top 100 since: 2001
See Ed's tip on page 112

HANK JOHNSON

Facility: Greystone G.C., Birmingham, Ala.
Website: www.greystonecc.com
Teaching since: 1969
Top 100 since: 1999

DARRELL KESTNER

Facility: Deepdale G.C., Manhasset, N.Y.
Website: www.deepdalegolfclub.com
Teaching since: 1980
Top 100 since: 1996
See Darrell's tip on page 122

CHARLIE KING

Facility: Reynolds Plantation, Greensboro, Ga.
Website: www.reynoldsgolfacademy.com
Teaching since: 1989
Top 100 since: 2003

PETER KOSTIS

Facility: Kostis/McCord Learning Center, Scottsdale, AZ
Website: www.kostismccordlearning.com
Teaching since: 1971
Top 100 since: 1996
See Peter's tips on pages 71, 160

DON KOTNIK

Facility: Toledo Country Club, Toledo, Ohio
Website: www.toledocountryclub.com
Teaching since: 1969
Top 100 since: 2005

PETER KRAUSE

Facility: Hank Haney International Junior Golf Academy, Hilton Head, S.C.
Website: www.peterkrausegolf.com
Teaching since: 1981
Top 100 since: 1999

MIKE LaBAUVE

Facility: Westin Kierland Resort and Spa, Scottsdale, Ariz.
Website: www.kierlandresort.com
Teaching since: 1980
Top 100 since: 1996

SANDY LaBAUVE

Facility: Westin Kierland Resort and Spa, Scottsdale, Ariz.
Website: www.kierlandresort.com
Teaching since: 1984
Top 100 since: 1996

ROD LIDENBERG

Facility: Prestwick G.C., Woodbury, Minn.
Website: www.pgamasterpro.com
Teaching since: 1972
Top 100 since: 2007
See Rod's tips on pages 105, 109, 178

MICHAEL LOPUSZYNSKI

Facility: David Glenz G.A., Franklin, N.J.
Website: www.davidglenz.com
Teaching since: 1987
Top 100 since: 1996
See Mike's tips on pages 27, 38, 62, 63, 114, 170

185

JACK LUMPKIN

Facility: Sea Island Golf Learning Center, St. Simons Island, Ga.
Website: www.seaisland.com
Teaching since: 1958
Top 100 since: 1996

KEITH LYFORD

Facility: Golf Academy at Old Greenwood, Truckee, Calif.
Website: www.lyfordgolf.cnet
Teaching since: 1982
Top 100 since: 1999

BILL MADONNA

Facility: Bill Madonna G.A, Orlando, Fla.
Website: www.marriottworldcenter.com
Teaching since: 1971
Top 100 since: 1996

TIM MAHONEY

Facility: Talking Stick G.C., Scottsdale, Ariz.
Website: www.timmahoneygolf.com
Teaching since: 1980
Top 100 since: 1996
See Tim's tip on page 133

MIKE MALASKA

Facility: Superstition Mt. G. & C.C., Superstition Mt., AZ
Website: www.malaskagolf.com
Teaching since: 1982
Top 100 since: 1996
See Mike's tip on page 142

CONTRIBUTORS

186

PAUL MARCHAND
Facility: Shadow Hawk G.C., Richmond, Tex.
Website: www.golfspan.com
Teaching since: 1981
Top 100 since: 1996

LYNN MARRIOTT
Facility: Coaching fir the Future, Phoenix, Ariz.
Website: www.golf54.com
Teaching since: 1982
Top 100 since: 1996

RICK MARTINO
Facility: PGA of America, Port St. Lucie, Fla.
Website: www.pgavillage.com
Teaching since: 1970
Top 100 since: 2003

RICK McCORD
Facility: McCord Golf Academy at Orange Lake Resort, Kissimmee, Fla.
Website: www.themccordgolfacademy.com
Teaching since: 1973
Top 100 since: 1996

GERALD McCULLAGH
Facility: University of Minnesota Le Bolstad G.C., Falcon Heights, Minn.
Website: www.uofmgolf.com
Teaching since: 1967
Top 100 since: 1996

MIKE McGETRICK
Facility: Mike McGetrick Golf Academy, Denver, Colo.
Website: www.mcgetrickgolf.com
Teaching since: 1983
Top 100 since: 1996

PATTI McGOWAN
Facility: Knack 4 Golf, Orlando, Fla.
Website: www.knack4golf.com
Teaching since: 1986
Top 100 since: 1996

JIM McLEAN
Facility: Jim McLean Golf School at Doral Golf Resort, Miami, Fla.
Website: www.jimmclean.com
Teaching since: 1975
Top 100 since: 1996

BRIAN MOGG
Facility: Brian Mogg Golf Performance Center at Golden Bear G.C., Windermere, Fla.
Website: www.moggperformance.com
Teaching since: 1992
Top 100 since: 2005

BILL MORETTI
Facility: Academy of Golf at the Hills of Lakeway, Austin, Tex.
Website: www.golfdynamics.com
Teaching since: 1979
Top 100 since: 1996

JERRY MOWLDS
Facility: Pumpkin Ridge G.C., North Plains, Or.
Website: www.pumpkinridge.com
Teaching since: 1970
Top 100 since: 1996
See Jerry's tip on page 161

JIM MURPHY
Facility: Jim Murphy Golf, Sugar Land, Tex.
Website: www.jimmurphygolf.com
Teaching since: 1984
Top 100 since: 2003
See Jim's tips on pages 20, 134

TOM NESS
Facility: Reunion Golf Club, Hoschton, Ga.
Website: www.chateauelanatlanta.com
Teaching since: 1972
Top 100 since: 2007

PIA NILSSON
Facility: Coaching fir the Future, Phoenix, Ariz.
Website: www.golf54.com
Teaching since: 1987
Top 100 since: 2001

DAN PASQUARIELLO
Facility: Pebble Beach Golf Academy, Pebble Beach, Calif.
Website: www.pebblebeach.com
Teaching since: 1970
Top 100 since: 2007

TOM PATRI
Facility: Friar's Head G.C., Baiting Hollow, N.Y.
Website: www.tompatri.com
Teaching since: 1981
Top 100 since: 2001
See Tom's tips on pages 32, 148, 156

BRUCE PATTERSON
Facility: Butler National G.C., Oak Brook, Ill.
Website: None
Teaching since: 1980
Top 100 since: 2005

MIKE PERPICH
Facility: RiverPines Golf, Alpharetta, Ga.
Website: www.mikeperpich.com
Teaching since: 1976
Top 100 since: 2001

GALE PETERSON
Facility: Sea Island Golf Learning Center, St. Simons Island, Ga.
Website: www.seaisland.com
Teaching since: 1978
Top 100 since: 1996

DAVID PHILLIPS
Facility: Titleist Performance Institute, Oceanside, Calif.
Website: www.titleistperformanceinstitute.com
Teaching since: 1989
Top 100 since: 2001

CAROL PREISINGER
Facility: Kiawah Island Club G.A., Kiawah Island, S.C.
Website: www.kiawahislandclub.com
Teaching since: 1986
Top 100 since: 2005
See Carol's tip on page 136

KIP PUTERBAUGH
Facility: Aviara Golf Academy, Carlsbad, Calif.
Website: www.aviaragolfacademy.com
Teaching since: 1972
Top 100 since: 1996

NANCY QUARCELINO
Facility: Nancy Quarcelino School of Golf, Spring Hill, Tenn.
Website: www.qsog.com
Teaching since: 1979
Top 100 since: 2003

CARL RABITO
Facility: Rabito Golf at Bolingbrook G.C., Bolingbrook, Ill.
Website: www.rabitogolf.com
Teaching since: 1987
Top 100 since: 2007

DANA RADER
Facility: Ballantyne Resort, Charlotte, N.C.
Website: www.danarader.com
Teaching since: 1980
Top 100 since: 1996
See Dana's tips on pages 51, 138, 144,

BRAD REDDING
Facility: The Resort Club at Grande Dunes, Myrtle Beach, S.C.
Website: www.grandedunes.com
Teaching since: 1984
Top 100 since: 2001

DEAN REINMUTH
Facility: Dean of Golf, San Diego, Calif.
Website: www.deanofgolf.com
Teaching since: 1978
Top 100 since: 1996

BRADY RIGGS
Facility: Woodley Lakes G.C., Van Nuys, Calif.
Website: www.bradyriggs.com
Teaching since: 1990
Top 100 since: 2007
See Brady's tips on pages 12-17, 54, 149, 150

SCOTT SACKETT
Facility: Resort Golf Schools, Scottsdale, Ariz.
Website: www.scottsackett.com
Teaching since: 1985
Top 100 since: 1999

TED SHEFTIC
Facility: Ted Sheftic Learning Center, Hanover, Pa.
Website: www.tedsheftic.com
Teaching since: 1966
Top 100 since: 2003
See Ted's tips on pages 24, 47, 56, 66, 162, 172

LAIRD SMALL
Facility: Pebble Beach Golf Academy,
Pebble Beach, Calif.
Website: www.pebblebeach.com
Teaching since: 1977
Top 100 since: 1996

RANDY SMITH
Facility: Royal Oaks C.C., Dallas, Tex.
Website: www.roccdallas.com
Teaching since: 1973
Top 100 since: 2001

RICK SMITH
Facility: Rick Smith Golf Academy at Tiburon,
Naples, Fla.
Website: www.ricksmith.com
Teaching since: 1977
Top 100 since: 1996

TODD SONES
Facility: Impact Golf Schools at White Deer Run G.C.,
Vernon Hills, Ill.
Website: www.toddsones.com
Teaching since: 1982
Top 100 since: 1996

CHARLES SORRELL
Facility: Sorrell School of Golf, Stockbridge, Ga.
Website: www.sorrellgolf.com
Teaching since: 1966
Top 100 since: 1996

MITCHELL SPEARMAN
Facility: Manhattan Woods G.C., West Nyack, N.Y.
Website: www.mitchellspearman.com
Teaching since: 1979
Top 100 since: 1996
See Mitchell's tip on page 108

TOM F. STICKNEY II
Facility: Bighorn Golf Club, Palm Desert, Calif.
Website: www.tomstickneygolf.com
Teaching since: 1990
Top 100 since: 2007

JON TATTERSALL
Facility: Golf Performance Partners, Atlanta, Ga.
Website: www.golfpp.com
Teaching since: 1986
Top 100 since: 2007

DR. T.J. TOMASI
Facility: Nantucket G.C., Siasconset, Mass.
Website: www.tjtomasi.com
Teaching since: 1975
Top 100 since: 1999

PAUL TRITTLER
Facility: Kostis/McCord Learning Ctr., Scottsdale, Ariz.
Website: www.kostismccordlearning.com
Teaching since: 1983
Top 100 since: 1999

J. D. TURNER
Facility: The Turner Golf Group, Savannah, Ga.
Website: www.jdturnergolf.com
Teaching since: 1965
Top 100 since: 1996

KEVIN WALKER
Facility: Fuzion Golf, Jupiter, Fla.
Website: www.fuziongolf.com
Teaching since: 1979
Top 100 since: 1996
See Kevin's tip on page 145

CARL WELTY, JR.
Facility: Jim McLean G.S. at PGA West, La Quinta, Calif.
Website: www.jimmclean.com/usa/pga-west
Teaching since: 1965
Top 100 since: 1996

CHUCK WINSTEAD
Facility: The University Club, Baton Rouge, La.
Website: www.universityclubbr.com
Teaching since: 1993
Top 100 since: 2005
See Chuck's tips on pages 70, 128

MARK WOOD
Facility: Cornerstone Club, Montrose, Colo.
Website: www.cornerstonecolorado.com
Teaching since: 1984
Top 100 since: 1999

DR. DAVID WRIGHT
Facility: Wright Balance Golf Academy,
Mission Viejo, Calif.
Website: www.wrightbalance.com
Teaching since: 1982
Top 100 since: 2005

187

Get more information on GOLF Magazine's Top 100 Teachers and the Top Teachers by region, plus exclusive video tips and drills at www.golf.com.

EMERITUS

The master class of the Top 100 Teachers in America: 500 years of teaching know-how

JIMMY BALLARD
Facility: Ballard Swing Connection,
Key Largo, Fla.
Website: www.jimmyballard.com
Teaching since: 1960
Top 100 since: 1996

PEGGY KIRK BELL
Facility: Pine Needles Resort,
Southern Pines, N.C.
Website: www.pineneedles-midpines.com
Teaching since: 1958
Top 100 since: 1996

CHUCK COOK
Facility: Chuck Cook Golf Academy at Barton Creek C.C., Austin, Tex.
Website: www.bartoncreek.com
Teaching since: 1975
Top 100 since: 1996

MANUEL DE LA TORRE
Facility: Milwaukee C.C., River Hills, Wis.
Website: www.manueldelatorregolf.com
Teaching since: 1948
Top 100 since: 1996

JIM FLICK
Facility: Desert Mountain Club,
Scottsdale, Ariz.
Website: www.jimflick.com
Teaching since: 1954
Top 100 since: 1996

MICHAEL HEBRON
Facility: Smithtown Landing G.C.,
Smithtown, N.Y.
Website: www.mikehebron.com
Teaching since: 1967
Top 100 since: 1996

DAVID LEADBETTER
Facility: David Leadbetter Golf Academy,
Champions Gate, Fla.
Website: www.davidleadbetter.com
Teaching since: 1976
Top 100 since: 1996

EDDIE MERRINS
Facility: Bel-Air C.C., Los Angeles, Calif.
Website: www.eddiemerrins.com
Teaching since: 1957
Top 100 since: 1996

DAVE PELZ
Facility: Pelz Golf, Austin, Tex.
Website: www.pelzgolf.com
Teaching since: 1976
Top 100 since: 1996
See Mr. Pelz's tip on page 141

PHIL RITSON
Facility: Phil Ritson Golf Your Way,
Winter Garden, Fla.
Website: www.ocngolf.com
Teaching since: 1950
Top 100 since: 1996

PHIL RODGERS
Facility: Carlton Oaks C.C., San Diego, Calif.
Website: None
Teaching since: 1977
Top 100 since: 1996

CRAIG SHANKLAND
Facility: Craig Shankland G.S.,
Daytona Beach, Fla.
Website: None
Teaching since: 1957
Top 100 since: 1996

DR. JIM SUTTIE
Facility: Suttie Academies at TwinEagles,
Naples, Fla.
Website: www.jimsuttie.com
Teaching since: 1972
Top 100 since: 1996

BOB TOSKI
Facility: Toski-Battersby Golf Learning Ctr.,
Coconut Creek, Fla.
Website: www.learn-golf.com
Teaching since: 1956
Top 100 since: 1996

DR. GARY WIREN
Facility: Trump Int., W. Palm Beach, Fla.
Website: www.garywiren.com
Teaching since: 1955
Top 100 since: 1996
See Dr. Wiren's tip on page 26

HOW TO HIT EVERY SHOT

OFF THE TEE

SHOT NAME	CLUB	AIM	STANCE	BALL POSITION	SWING	FEEL	PAGE #
Power draw (1)	Driver	Right of center	Square to aim line	Standard	Full	Swing out to the right	20
Power fade (2)	Driver	Left of center	Square to aim line	Slightly forward of standard	Full back to full finish	Hit the outside lower quadrant of the ball	22
Extra-high drive (3)	Driver	At target	Extra-wide	Off left toe	Full	Stay over right side throughout	24
Low drive (4)	Driver	At target	Standard	Slightly back (off shirt logo)	Full back to full finish	Like you're swinging at 80-percent speed	26
Stinger long iron (5)	3-iron	At target	Slightly open	Slightly back	Three-quarter back to full finish	Like your wrists are stiff at impact	27
Driving the green (6)	Driver	At target	Standard	Standard	Standard	Confidence—you'll get this on!	28
Angled tee box (7)	Driver	At target	Parallel to target line	Standard	Full back to full finish	Drill it over intermediate target	29
The big bomb (8)	Driver	At target	Standard	Standard	Big turn back, fast turn through	Your wrists are soft and tension-free	30
Super-accurate drive (9)	Driver	At target	Square to target	Slightly back of standard	Full back to full finish	Like it's an elongated pitch shot	32

FROM THE FAIRWAY

SHOT NAME	CLUB	AIM	STANCE	BALL POSITION	SWING	FEEL	PAGE #
Ball above feet (10)	+1 club	10 yards left of target	Standard	Standard	At 80-percent power	Like you're swinging a baseball bat	36
Ball below feet (11)	+1 club	Slightly left of target	Feet outside shoulders	Standard	At 70-percent speed	Stay in your address posture	38
Ball severely below feet (12)	Mid-iron	10 yards left of target	Weight on heels	Center	Vertical and full back and through	Your chest is on top of the ball	40
Ball severely above feet (13)	+1 club	15 yards right of target	Weight on toes	Center	Flat and full back and through	Swing right arm across your chest	41
From an upslope (14)	+2 clubs	Slightly right of target	Extra wide	Slightly forward of standard	Three-quarter back to ¾ finish	You're hitting the shot with all arms	42
From a downslope (15)	-1 club	At target	Body tilted to slope	Slightly back of standard	Full back to a low finish	Swing back the slope, then down the slope	44
From a severe upslope (16)	+1 club	Slightly right of target	Body tilted to slope	One ball forward of center	Full back to a high finish	Like you're hanging back on your right side	46
From a severe downslope (17)	+1 club	Right of target	Right foot pulled back	Standard	Three quarters to maintain balance	Like you're swinging high to very low	47
Upslope, ball above feet (18)	+2 clubs	10 yards right of target	Hips tilted and tucked	Toward left foot	Full back to three-quarter finish	Swing follows your hips	48
Downslope, ball below feet (19)	Variable	Slightly left of target	Hips tilted and back	Toward left foot	At 60-percent power	Let the club release after impact	49
Downhill approach (20)	-1 for 30-ft drop	At target	Standard	Standard	Full (shorter club); ¾ (longer club)	Know your actual distance	50
Uphill approach (21)	+1 for 30-ft rise	At target	Standard	Standard	Full back to full finish	Hit the bottom of the ball	52
Ball in a divot (22)	Variable	Standard	Standard	Two inches inside right heel	Full back to ¼ finish	Hands stay in front of club from start to finish	54
100-yard shot (23)	Pitching wedge	At target	Standard	Standard	From 9 o'clock to 12 o'clock	You're swinging around a clock	56
80-yard shot (24)	Gap wedge	At target	Standard	Standard	From 9 o'clock to 2 o'clock	You're swinging around a clock	56
60-yard shot (25)	Sand wedge	At target	Standard	Standard	From 10 o'clock to 12 o'clock	You're swinging around a clock	56
In-between clubs (26)	Variable	At target	Standard	Back (short iron), forward (long iron)	Full (shorter iron), 3/4 (longer iron)	Same pace despite different swing lengths	58
Low draw (27)	Variable	Clubface at target	Right of target	Between center and right foot	Full backswing to full finish	Keep your forearms soft to turn the ball over	60
High draw (28)	Variable	Clubface at target	Right of target	Slightly forward	At 85-percent speed	Longer swing with more release	62
High fade (29)	Variable	Clubface at target	Left of target	Between center and left heel	At full speed	Like you're holding the face open at impact	63
Low fade (30)	Variable	Clubface at target	Left of target	Between center and right foot	Three-quarters to three-quarters	Like you're holding the face open at impact	64
To a back pin (31)	Variable	Variable	Variable	Variable	Variable	Confidence in your selection	65
Against the wind (32)	+1 for 10-mph wind	At target	Standard	Off right foot	Compact back and through	Firm left arm through impact	68
With a crosswind (33)	Variable	Left (fade); Std. (draw)	Standard	Back (draw); forward (fade)	Standard	Roll left forearm through impact (draw)	68
With the wind (34)	-1 for 10-mph wind	At target	Tilt upper body to right	One ball's width forward	Full back to full finish	Smooth, easy tempo	69
Long-iron approach (35)	Long iron	Standard	Shoulder-width	Between center and left foot	Full back to full finish	Right shoulder down, high hands at finish	70
Carry over water (36)	Variable	Standard	Standard	Variable	Full back to full finish	Pinch the ball against the turf	71
Lay-up shot (37)	Variable	At target	Variable	Variable	Variable	Treat lay-ups like regular shots	72
Par-3 attack (38)	Variable	At best scatter area	Variable	Variable	Variable	Confidence—you picked the right spot	74
Wet ground (46)	Variable	At target	Standard	Center	Full back to full finish	Aim for the grass in front of the ball	88
Driver off the deck (92)	Driver	Slighlty left of target	Just like your 3-wood	Between center and left heel	Full with a shallow approach	Like you're just brushing the grass	170

188

Here are all the moves you need to hit the ball at your target from every lie

OFF THE FAIRWAY

SHOT NAME	CLUB	AIM	STANCE	BALL POSITION	SWING	FEEL	PAGE #
Against-the-grain rough (39)	+1 club	At target	Closer to ball, open face	Slightly back of standard	Steep going back and through	Point your thumbs at sky going back	76
With-the-grain rough (40)	-1 club	At target	Standard	Slightly forward of standard	Steep going back and through	Carry the ball short then let it roll	77
Gnarly rough escape (41)	Mid-iron	Standard	Shoulder-width	Center	Full back to full finish	Steep backswing, cut downswing	80
Deep rough escape (42)	Wedge or 9-iron	Right of target	Stand closer to ball	Between center and right foot	Full backswing, minimal follow-through	Pull the handle down hard from the top	82
Hardpan (43)	Hybrid or lofted FW	At target	Weight slightly on left side	Center	Three-quarter back to full finish	Hit the ball and dirt at same time	84
Cart path (44)	Any iron	Slightly left of target	Slightly open	Center	Favor balance over speed	Practice "nipping" the grass	86
Pine straw (45)	Variable	At target	Standard	Standard	Try to sweep it	Your feet are in cement	87
Feet in bunker, ball on grass (47)	Sand wedge	Left of target	Open	Slightly back of center	Wristy backswing, low follow-through	Point clubface at sky through impact	90
Restricted forward-swing (48)	Short to mid-iron	Standard	Shoulder-width	As close to center as possible	Half back, stop at impact	Pull back the club like it hit a tire after impact	92
Restricted backswing (49)	Short iron	At target	Square to target; narrow	Slightly left of center	At 60-percent speed	Brush the ground in your practice swings	94
Through the trees (50)	Mid- to long iron	Standard	Shoulder-width	Back of center	Half back to half finish	Flat swing with a strong release	96
Over an obstacle (51)	+1 club	At target	Open (fade stance)	Slightly forward of standard	Full back to full finish	Fold arms quickly after impact	98
From your knees (52)	Hybrid or FW	At target	From your knees	Center	Baseball-type swing	Lead the clubhead with your hands	100
Mega-hook (93)	Mid-iron	40 yards right	Right foot back	Center	Full back to full finish	Normal, everyday motion	172
Mega-slice (94)	Mid-iron	40 yards left	Left foot back	Off left heel	Full back to full finish	Normal, everyday motion	173
Left-handed save (95)	Sand wedge	Toward safety	Left-handed	Off left foot	Putting stroke	Smooth stroke to advance it ten yards	174
Back-handed save (96)	Any wedge	Toward safety	Back facing target	To the side of right foot	Up-and-down slap shot	Like you're doing a triceps pull-down exercise	175

FROM THE SAND

SHOT NAME	CLUB	AIM	STANCE	BALL POSITION	SWING	FEEL	PAGE #
Standard bunker shot (53)	Sand wedge	Slightly left of target	Slightly open	Between center and left foot	Full back to full finish	"Splash" the ball out	104
Plugged lie (54)	Sand wedge	At target	Square, weight forward	Between center and left foot	Full to impact then stop	Bury the club in the sand	106
Fried egg (55)	Sand wedge	Slightly left of target	Slightly open	Between center and left foot	Full swing with lots of wrist hinge	Like you're coming down too steep	108
Semi-buried (56)	Sand wedge	Square clubface	Narrow, weight on left foot	Back of center	Three-quarters to three-quarters	Firm hands	109
Hard sand (57)	Sand wedge	At target	Standard	Standard	Slower (shorter swing)	Swing hip-high to hip-high	110
Fluffy sand (58)	Sand wedge	At target	Standard	Standard	Faster (longer swing)	Swing shoulder-high to full finish	110
Wet sand (59)	Lob wedge	Open clubface	Wide, weight over left	Center	From three-quarter back to full finish	Accelerate though impact	112
From an upslope (60)	Sand wedge	At target	Open, match slope	Slightly forward	Full back to full finish	Hit up the slope	114
From a downslope (61)	Sand wedge	At target	Left foot dug in more	Off right heel	Half back to half through	Like you're swinging down the slope	116
Ball above feet (62)	Sand wedge	Way right of target	Square to aim line	Under logo of shirt	Full bunker motion	Swing around your spine	118
Ball below feet (63)	Sand wedge	Slightly left of target	Square to aim line	Under logo of shirt	Full bunker motion	Keep your knees flexed	120
Against the lip (64)	Lob wedge	Left of target	Open, weight over left foot	Slightly right of center	Full to impact then stop	A shallow downswing, like you're skipping stones	122
Flop from sand (65)	Lob wedge	Standard	Standard	Off left heel	Half backswing, three-quarter finish	Flip clubhead past hands at impact	124
40-yard bunker shot (66)	SW (blast); PW (pick)	Slightly left of target	Standard (but don't dig in)	Left heel (blast); left thigh (pick)	Three-quarter (blast); knee-high (pick)	Enter sand before (blast) or after (pick) the ball	126
Fairway bunker (67)	+1 club	Slightly left of target	Don't dig feet in	Center	Three-quarter back to full finish	Quiet legs on downswing	129
One foot in bunker (97)	Lob or sand wedge	Standard	Closed, right foot out	Forward of standard	At 50-percent speed	Swing down the slope	176
Bunker punch-out (98)	6-, 7- or 8-iron	At target	Narrow, weight on left side	Slightly right of center	Half back to half through	Firm wrists at impact	178
Bunker chip-out (99)	9-, 8- or 7-iron	At target	Feet close together	Center	Chipping motion	Hit the ball then the sand	180

APPROACH WITH THE BALL ABOVE YOUR FEET
Shot 10 *[page 36]*
Follow Top 100 Teacher Anne Cain's advice to easily beat the most common uneven lie.

40-YARD BUNKER BLAST
Shot 66 *[page 126]*
Top 100 Teacher David Glenz provides not one, but two ways to get it close from this tough distance.

PAR SAVE FROM YOUR KNEES
Shot 52 *[page 100]*
Tree trouble? Then drop down and give Top 100 Teacher Jason Carbone's knee-high swing a go.

AROUND THE GREEN

SHOT NAME	CLUB	AIM	STANCE	BALL POSITION	SWING	FEEL	PAGE #
Long pitch (68)	9-iron	Left of target	Narrow	Slightly back of center	Half back to half through	Pull down with your left arm	132
Chip over an obstacle (69)	Any wedge	At target	Narrow	Center	Half back to half through	Swing left of target after impact	133
One-hop-and-stop pitch (70)	Sand wedge	At target	Weight forward	Off left foot	Half back to half through	"Pinch" the ball against the ground	134
Bump-and-run (71)	7- or 8-iron	At target	Open, weight over left foot	Slightly right of center	Thigh-high back to hip-high finish	You're stroking a long putt	136
Short-sided chip (72)	SW, GW or LW	Standard	Variable	Variable	Variable	See wrist action notes	138
Chip from tight lie (73)	Any wedge	At target	Standard	Between center and right foot	Weight over left leg throughout	Like you're on a seesaw tilted left	140
Chip from a downslope (74)	Sand wedge	At target	Right foot pulled back	Off right heel	Along the slope	Release the club like a full swing	142
Chip from an upslope (75)	+1 club	Standard	Weight favors right foot	Between center and left heel	Standard chip	Hands and clubhead finishing low	144
Chip from hardpan (76)	Gap or pitch wedge	Standard	Weight favors left foot	Between center and left heel	Aggressive chip	Swing down, glove logo points at target	145
Chip from rough (77)	Sand wedge	Standard	Farther from ball	Center, back (low) or forward (high)	At 75-percent force	Club skips under the ball	146
Chip from deep rough (78)	Sand or lob wedge	Standard	Well-balanced	Slightly forward of center	At 50-percent speed	Fluid—the club should glide through the grass	147
Flop shot (79)	Lob wedge	Shade left of target	Slightly open	Slightly forward	Three-quarters to full	Quiet hands	148
Ball against fringe (80)	Pitching wedge	At target	Standard putting stance	Off left heel	Straight-back-and-through stroke	Like you're thinning it on purpose	150
Chip from fringe (81)	Sand wedge	Left of target	Standard chipping stance	Just forward of center	Standard chip motion	Regular speed with a choke grip	151
Bank-shot chip (91)	Mid-iron	At target	Feet inside shoulders	One half-ball back of center	At 70-percent speed	Hard chip	168
High chip off hardpan (101)	Lob wedge	Slightly left of target	Slightly open	One inch back of center	Aggressive chop	Like you're keeping the face open at impact	182

ON THE GREEN

SHOT NAME	CLUB	AIM	STANCE	BALL POSITION	SWING	FEEL	PAGE #
100-foot putt (82)	Putter	Standard	Standard	Slightly back	Long pendulum	Imitate practice strokes	154
Uphill putt (83)	Putter	Read from low side	Wider than normal	Slightly back of center	Standard	Make a level blow	156
Downhill putt (84)	Putter	At the "speed spot"	Weight on front foot	Center	Pendulum-like	Total commitment	157
Down a tier (85)	Putter	At intermediate target	Standard	Standard	Standard	Roll the ball to the cusp	158
Up a tier (86)	Putter	At target	Standard	Standard	Standard	"Bowl" the ball up to the tier	159
Double-breaker (87)	Putter	At the turning point	Standard	Standard	Standard	Trust in your read	160
On windy days (88)	Putter	At target	Feet outside shoulders	Center	Standard	Like you're "braced" against the wind	161
Lag putt (89)	Putter	At target	Standard	Standard	Practice stroke looking at hole	Same speed, different backstroke lengths	162
Short breaking putt (90)	Putter	Variable	Standard	Standard	Standard	Picture the roll—then do it	164

Time Inc. HOME ENTERTAINMENT

PUBLISHER
Richard Fraiman

GENERAL MANAGER
Steven Sandonato

EXECUTIVE DIRECTOR, MARKETING SERVICES
Carol Pittard

DIRECTOR, RETAIL & SPECIAL SALES
Tom Mifsud

DIRECTOR, NEW PRODUCT DEVELOPMENT
Peter Harper

ASSISTANT DIRECTOR, BRAND MARKETING
Laura Adam

ASSOCIATE COUNSEL
Helen Wan

SENIOR BRAND MANAGER, TWRS/M
Holly Oakes

BRAND & LICENSING MANAGER
Alexandra Bliss

DESIGN & PREPRESS MANAGER
Anne-Michelle Gallero

BOOK PRODUCTION MANAGER
Susan Chodakiewicz

THANK YOU
Mike Beck, Glenn Buonocore, Caroline DeNunzio, F. David DeNunzio III, Noelle Ewen, Shayna Halper, Rob Hammer, Margaret Hess, Suzanne Janso, Robert Marasco, Dennis Marcel, Jessica Marksbury, Evan Michals, Dennis Murphy, Brooke Reger, Jesse Reiter, Mary Sarro-Waite, Ilene Schreider, Dennis Scully, Adriana Tierno, Alex Voznesenskiy, Kris Widger, Ken Yagoda.

GOLF MAGAZINE

EDITOR
David M. Clarke

CREATIVE DIRECTOR
Paul Crawford

DEPUTY EDITOR
Michael Corcoran

ART DIRECTOR
Paul Ewen

MANAGING EDITOR (INSTRUCTION)
David DeNunzio

CONTENT DEVELOPMEENT EDITOR
Eamon Lynch

EDITOR AT LARGE
Connell Barrett

SENIOR EDITOR
Michael Walker

PRODUCTION EDITOR
Gary Perkinson

DEPUTY ART DIRECTOR
Karen Ha

ASSOCIATE PHOTO EDITOR
Carrie Boretz

PUBLISHER
Charles R. Kammerer

ASSOCIATE PUBLISHER
Nathan Stamos

DIRECTOR OF BUSINESS DEVELOPMNET
Brad J. Felenstein

GENERAL MANAGER
Kerry Murphy

NATIONAL DIRECTOR OF ONLINE SALES
Bill Keating

VICE PRESIDENT OF CONSUMER MARKETING
John Kerner

Sports Illustrated

GOLF Magazine is published in conjunction with *Sports Illustrated*

PRESIDENT/PUBLISHER
Mark Ford

EDITOR
Terry McDonell

VICE PRESIDENT, GENERAL MANAGER
Oliver Knowlton

PRESIDENT, SI DIGITAL
Jeff Price

DEPUTY MANAGING EDITOR
David Bauer

EXECUTIVE EDITORS
Michael Bevans
Charlie Leehsen

CHIEF MARKETING OFFICER
Andrew R. Judelson

ASSOCIATE PUBLISHER
Richard A. Raskopf

ASSISTANT MANAGING EDITORS
Neil Cohen (SI Presents)
James P. Herre (Golf Plus/golf.com)
Craig Neff

191

GOLF.com

EXECUTIVE EDITOR
Charlie Hanger

DEPUTY EDITOR
David Dusek

PRODUCERS
Ryan Reiterman
Anne Szeker

CREDITS

WORDS

THE TOP 100 TEACHERS IN AMERICA
with
DAVID DeNUNZIO
MICHAEL WALKER

DESIGN

PAUL EWEN

ILLUSTRATION

ROBIN GRIGGS 28, 65, 72-73, 132

BARRY ROSS 53, 60-61, 64, 95, 132, 151, 181

PHOTOGRAPHY

BOB ATKINS 12-17, 54-55, 138-139, 144, 149 [R], 150

NEIL BECKERMAN 137 [R]

DAVID BERGMAN 145

D2 PRODUCTIONS 20-21, 30, 31 [L], 33 [R], 37 [R], 40-41, 44-46, 52-53, 68-70, 73 [M], 76-77, 84-85, 86, 88-89, 100, 101 [L], 116-117, 121 [R], 123 [R], 128, 129 [L], 134-135, 140, 142-143, 158-159, 161, 175 [R]

DARREL ESTRINE 25, 73, 83, 101, 113, 129 [Rules]

SAM GREENWOOD 87

LEONARD KAMSLER 90-91, 98-99, 108, 122, 123 [L], 182-183

SCHECTER LEE 22-25 [L], 27, 29, 32-33, 42-43, 47-51, 56-59, 62-63, 66-67, 74-75, 82, 83 [L], 104, 105 [L], 110-111, 118-121 [L], 124-125, 136, 137 [L], 141 [L], 147 [R], 148, 149 [L], 156-157, 162-165, 170-174, 175 [L]

ANGUS MURRAY 2-3, 6-7, 8, 10-11, 18-19, 26, 31 [BR], 34-36, 37 [L], 38-39, 78-81, 92-95, 102-103, 105 [R], 106-107, 109, 112, 113 [L], 114-115, 126-127, 130-131, 146, 147 [L], 152-155, 166-169, 176-180, 192

MICHAEL O'BRIEN 141 [R]

MARC SEROTA 96-97

FRED VUICH 71, 160

Time Inc.
HOME ENTERTAINMENT

GOLF
MAGAZINE

Time Inc.
HOME ENTERTAINMENT

Copyright 2008
Time Inc. Home Entertainment

Some of the material in this book was previously published in *GOLF Magazine*, and is reprinted with permission by Time Inc.

Published by Time Inc. Home Entertainment

Time Inc.
1271 Avenue of the Americas
New York, New York 10020

ISBN 10: 1-60320-038-X
ISBN 13: 978-1-60320-038-7
Library of Congress Control Number: 2008903292

Printed in China

We welcome your comments and suggestions about Time Inc. Home Entertainment Books.
Please write to us at:
Time Inc. Home Entertainment Books
Attention: Book Editors
PO Box 11016
Des Moines, IA 50336-1016

If you would like to order any of our hardcover Collector's Edition books, please call us at 1-800-327-6388.
(Monday through Friday, 7:00 a.m. — 8:00 p.m. or Saturday, 7:00 a.m. — 6:00 p.m. Central Time).

Cover and book design by Paul Ewen
Cover photographs by D2 Productions, Schecter Lee, Angus Murray, Marc Serota